W9-ASJ-639

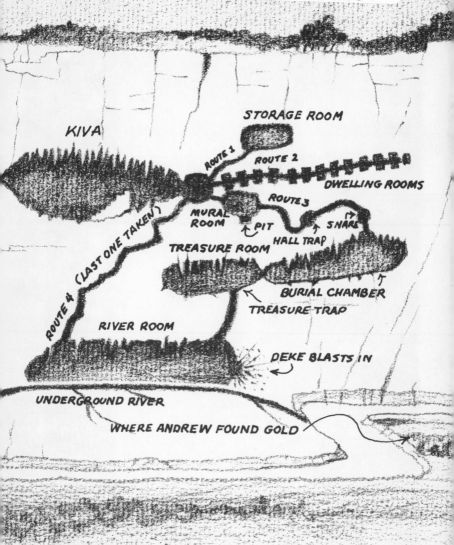

KIVA

STORAGE ROOM

ROUTE 1

ROUTE 2

DWELLING ROOMS

ROUTE 3

MURAL ROOM

PIT

SNARE

HALL TRAP

TREASURE ROOM

BURIAL CHAMBER

ROUTE 4 (LAST ONE TAKEN)

TREASURE TRAP

RIVER ROOM

DEKE BLASTS IN

UNDERGROUND RIVER

WHERE ANDREW FOUND GOLD

SERPENT TREASURE

SERPENT
TREASURE

SUELLEN R. McDANIEL

JOHN F. BLAIR, PUBLISHER
Winston-Salem, North Carolina

Library of Congress Cataloging in Publication Data
McDaniel, Suellen R
    Serpent treasure.
    SUMMARY: The fascinating legend of the lost Aztec
civilization and its golden treasure draws 16-year-old
Chris and his father to a rocky Texas canyon.
    [1. Aztecs—Fiction. 2. Indians of Mexico—Fiction.
3. Buried treasure—Fiction. 4. Mystery and
detective stories] 1. Title.
PZ7.M1415Se   [Fic]   78–24288
ISBN 0–89587–007–X

To JIM

PROLOGUE: 1522

ON A SUN-SCORCHED APRIL DAY IN THE year 1522, a straggling line of determined, plodding men and women wound, for half a mile behind their leader, along a man-made trail in the Texas desert. They wore once-proud but now bedraggled feathers in their smooth black hair, and the ragged covering of their sun-bronzed bodies was slight. They walked unsteadily but with the determination of those who use the last dregs of their energy to make an effort one last time. The pack-bearers staggered beneath their heavy loads and stumbled frequently among thick clusters of sagebrush. The smaller children were too tired to walk and lay exhausted across the shoulders of their parents.

The tall, young warrior who led them waited patiently for his people to catch up. To the west loomed the blue of distant mountains, the clear, thin air making them seem closer than they really were. The spring rains, now gone, had brought a short-lived brilliance to the cactuses. Their yellow, orange, and purple blooms were already fading in the sun. The pleasing green of an occasional mesquite mingled with the natural reds and yellows in outcroppings of desert rock. But the leader was the only one to see the beauty of the land around them.

He looked behind him at the weary tribe which had followed him through desert dust and wind for many months to leave the sounds of bloody battle far behind and to preserve their heritage intact. He watched the pack-carriers bear up beneath the pressure of their heavy loads, and once he caught the sun-sparked flash of gold from a carelessly tied bundle. He smiled with grim satisfaction, remembering the silence of his brave young chieftain as his Spanish captors tortured him to make him tell where the Indians had hidden the sacred treasure. But this band had managed to elude its tormentors long ago.

The tired, brown faces of his people were parched with the dry heat, and their swollen lips were cracked with thirst. It had been several hours since they had run out of water. They walked with their heads bowed, shielding their faces from a merciless sun. They had walked thus for many days, and the warrior knew that he was now the only one to see the miracle ahead, the sight that had caused him to stop and wait for the band to catch up. He turned his head to see the miracle again.

Before him lay a mighty chasm in the earth, which twisted through dust and rock like a giant, writhing serpent at his feet. The sparkling water of a turquoise river invited him to place his feet upon a narrow ledge of rock that formed a path along sheer cliffs and wound down to the water's edge far below. The banks of that distant river promised irrigation for crops grown from the seeds they had carried from their native land.

He saw the movement of a desert rabbit behind a bush on the trail below and knew that the canyon animals would provide fine quarry for his hunters. The barren walls of the cliffs across the river had been cut and carved by the elements in geometric brilliance, and they flashed like jewels in the noonday sun. A series of black openings caught his eye, and he thought what fine dwelling places the caves would make for the families of his tribe as shelter and protection from the thoughts and deeds of evil men.

Again he looked behind him at his people. The endless hardship they had faced to get this far had caused their number to diminish from death, desertion, and exhaustion. The fallen seed of his tribe would grow in many clusters on the trail behind, from those who had had no further strength to travel and had chosen to settle down where they had reached the limits of their courage.

He looked down at the canyon. He knew this was as far as they could go and still survive. He made the sign of the serpent, his tribe's protector, above the empty drop beneath his hand and said to those who reached the edge beside him, "This will be our home."

ONE

TWO TALL FIGURES STOOD BESIDE
their dusty jeep at the awesome precipice of Cougar
Canyon and surveyed the mighty chasm far below. The
aqua Pecos River sparkled in the noonday winter sunlight at the bottom of the gorge and hummed and spun
its way between the silent cliffs as it had done for thousands of years to split the earth and reach one thousand
feet in depth.

Below them, they saw a wooden cabin, made small
by distance and the overwhelming contrast of the majestic cliffs which framed it. It sat firmly on a ledge of
rock high above the calmly flowing water but far below
the sheer walls of the cliff, protected from the flashflood-
ing that was common to such canyons during the rainy
season. The distant structure's wooden deck curved
around the cabin in three directions; from it, one could
see for miles along the giant rock walls before the canyon curved and closed the view. Below the structure,
two animals, a mule and a horse, the cabin owner's only
sensible transportation in this wilderness, grazed on the
vegetation that sprouted from the rocky slope.

The elder of the two was Tom O'Reilly, a tall, slender man of forty-two and father of the boy beside him. At sixteen years of age, Chris O'Reilly was tall and strong and tan from continuous exposure to the sun. They looked like father and son, thought Tom, but not from physical resemblance. Instead, their kinship was apparent in their comradeship, an understanding that nothing could disturb. He himself was tall and tanned and blond. His son Chris was also tall and tanned, but his hair was dark brown. Only their eyes achieved a sameness . . . a clear, bright green which, as they looked down at the canyon, sparkled with excitement and anticipation.

Chris adjusted the climbing equipment he carried in a pack on his back and grinned at his father. "What did you say about going on 'a little climbing trip'?"

"Not too difficult for seasoned climbers like us." Tom smiled as he looked down at the cabin below. "Twenty-five years ago, I spent a summer here and made a lifelong friend. The man who lives in that cabin is a prospector, one of the few old-timers left in that time-honored profession but more special than most. His life is wrapped up in the search for a hidden piece of history." His face became serious as he looked at the lonely cabin.

"You're worried about him, aren't you, Dad?" asked Chris.

His father nodded. "Every six months for the past twenty-four years or so, Andrew Mahler has come into town for provisions. This is the first time he's failed to come by my office to see me. He was due two weeks ago. I did some checking with the stores he normally visits, and no one remembers doing business with him lately. Andrew's getting on in years, and this life he's

6

chosen is pretty hard. He may be ill or . . . ." His words ended before the thought was spoken, but they both knew what he meant.

"If he's as old as you say, why does he live here instead of in the city?" wondered Chris.

Tom smiled. "Andrew himself will have to tell you why he stays, but I can tell you the legend behind his reason."

"What's he looking for . . . a lost gold mine?" His son looked skeptically down the long descent and shook his head. "A couple of lifetimes wouldn't be enough to explore this chasm."

Tom nodded. "I know. He's here because of a legend passed down to him by his father and his grandfather before that. I'm going to tell it to you now. I first heard it when I was your age and spent the most exciting summer of my life down there looking for a trace of the treasure."

He sat down at the rocky edge of the canyon and motioned Chris to do the same. He looked ten years younger, as if the times he remembered in this place were fond memories. "If he's not sick or injured, Andrew must have had his reasons for not keeping his usual appointment with me. He was always a man who had good reasons for everything he did. I'll tell you the legend that has kept him here ever since he was a young man just starting out in life.

"About 450 years ago," he began, "a powerful civilization flourished in Mexico. They called themselves the Aztecs and lived in a beautiful city on an island in the middle of a lake. These people worshiped the sun, which gave them warmth and light and made their crops grow

7

tall. They were a wealthy people, and rumors spread far and wide of the fabulous golden treasure they possessed."

Deep in his story, he didn't seem to see the golden walls across the river sparkle with hypnotic brilliance which held his son's attention.

"Then the Spanish general Cortez heard of the gold in the New World and set sail with a great army to conquer the Indians and capture the treasure." Tom glanced significantly at his son's interested face.

"When Cortez met the Aztecs, he knew that the best way to conquer them was to win their friendship first. There were too many thousands of Indians for the Spanish soldiers ever to defeat in a battle, so he acted in a friendly way and tried to trick them into his control.

"But the Spaniards and Aztecs were much too different ever to be friends even in a pretending sort of way. The Indians' religious customs were so horrible to Cortez that he ordered them to change their religion and worship in the Spanish way.

"One night, when Cortez was away visiting another Indian city, some of his soldiers murdered a large number of Aztecs. The Indians could take no more. All of their hatred against the Spaniards burst into flame, and the fighting grew terrible indeed. When Cortez hurried back to the island city to help his men, he easily entered the city. But it was a trap. Once all the soldiers were inside, the Aztecs surrounded the city and wouldn't let them out again. They meant to destroy the Spaniards for good."

His voice grew softer. "It was a summer night in 1520. Cortez knew he had one chance to escape. The bridges leading to the city had been destroyed in the

8

fighting, but he ordered his men to make another bridge as well as they could from whatever they could find. When they were ready to leave, Cortez ordered them to collect part of the treasure for their king, but he saw that there was still a great treasure left. He told his soldiers they could take anything they wanted, but he warned them it was difficult to fight wearing heavy packs of gold. Some of the men listened to his advice and took only a little gold for themselves. But most of them were greedy. They loaded themselves down with treasure.

"As the men crossed the makeshift bridge to escape from the city, suddenly the Aztec warriors were everywhere. The Spaniards panicked and tore at the heavy packs to free their arms for the battle. They dropped the gold on the bridge in the darkness, thinking that someday they would return and capture it again. At last, outnumbered in the dark, Cortez and his soldiers managed to find their way across the lake, losing many of their men and horses on the way."

"But I thought Cortez won all his battles," said Chris, puzzled.

"Not this one. In fact, it was such a setback that historians call it the *noche triste*, the night of sorrows. But Cortez won the next battles against other towns and grew strong again. One year later, after a long siege, the soldiers returned to the island city to search for the gold."

"And it wasn't there," said Chris softly.

"Cortez was a very disappointed man, to put it lightly," agreed Tom. "When they finally captured the island capital, they found that the bulk of the gold had vanished, and only by searching the bottom of the lake were they able to recover a very small portion of the treasure. Cortez tortured the young Indian leader, but the brave warrior never told the secret of the gold."

"The Aztecs had recovered it and hidden it from their enemies. Smart Indians," said Chris approvingly.

For a moment, Tom O'Reilly let his eyes wander down the face of the cliff to the black holes of caves across from him. "In a manner of speaking, they did hide it," he answered at last, lowering his voice to give emphasis to his words. "According to the legend, which I first heard twenty-five years ago from Andrew, the Indians took the gold with them when they escaped. With their belongings and as much of the treasure as they could carry, several groups of Indians traveled up from Mexico into Texas, looking for a home where they would be safe from marauders and where food and shelter would be plentiful. They found such a place here—in the land now known as Texas."

"Here?" Chris raised an eyebrow.

Tom smiled at his son and nodded. "They were tired of running and stopped here after a terrible, heartbreaking journey during which they had lost many of their band. The seclusion of these walls must have looked pretty good to them."

"If the gold is still here," asked Chris curiously, "where did the Indians go, and why didn't they take it with them?"

"The rest of the story will come from Andrew himself. So let's get started; it's a long climb down." Tom rose to his feet and rubbed his left leg to get the circulation going.

Chris looked doubtfully across at him. "Dad, are

you sure your leg is strong enough for this climb?" he asked. "We've never tried a wall like this before."

Tom smiled and stretched and grinned. "I've had this limp for twenty-five years, and my leg always goes wherever I take it without too much complaining. Watch that first step, though; it's a big one."

TWO

THE FIRST IMPRESSION MOST PEOPLE had of Andrew Mahler was a flash of blue and white: blue for his wide-set azure eyes, which perfectly reflected the blue of the clear sky above the canyon; white for the spun sugar of his hair, the windblown white of constant, decades-long exposure to the sun. It grew long about his age-lined neck and was cut haphazardly, here and there, as if it didn't matter much so long as it didn't interfere with living. The lines of a thousand smiles had grown deep around his mouth, and now they cracked into curving chasms as he grinned at Tom O'Reilly.

"So you're back, young Tom. Took your time about it, didn't you?" The large eyes twinkled as they surveyed the equipment stacked against the rail of the long porch. "Looks like you figure on doing a bit of climbing. Haven't forgotten how, have you?" he teased, extending a large, rough hand in greeting.

They could see that to Andrew time was different, unimportant, here in the canyon. It might have been yesterday he'd talked with Tom O'Reilly, not six months before.

"I've been worried about you, my friend." The way Tom gripped the old man's hand left no room for doubt that he indeed valued his friendship. "You're late coming into town for the first time since I've known you."

Andrew's eyes avoided his. "There's a reason, Tom. I'll tell it to you later." His face brightened. "Who is this tall young man you've brought with you? As if I can't guess!"

"This is my son Chris." Tom smiled back. "I've told him that you know more about this canyon than any man alive, and he's going to ask you a thousand questions about the legend. He's as curious as I was the first time I came to see you."

Tom's relief that his friend was in good health was tempered by concern; but he saw that Andrew was reluctant to discuss his problem, so he didn't press the issue. All in good time. His friend knew that if he needed help he only had to ask.

The old miner paused in the act of pouring steaming mugs of coffee. The arc of the sun had passed the rim of the westward canyon wall and left the chasm in deep, chilly shadow. Although the rocks, which had felt the sun for several hours, were still warm to the touch, the air was colder now.

Andrew gave the boy a measured look. "How much has your father told you about the canyon's history?"

"He stopped about the time the Aztecs decided to settle down here." Chris grinned and shook his head. "Dad likes to keep me in suspense." He looked across at the dark, empty holes in the rock. "It's pretty certain they didn't wait for us to get here."

Andrew eyed Chris thoughtfully. "They were gone

13

long before my grandfather first heard the story. My father never traced them either. I've broken that tradition." He laughed softly, and it was the most satisfied expression of a life well spent they'd ever heard.

He gestured to the waiting walls of rock, silent but for the music of the flowing river below. "Somewhere, hidden beneath all that rock, is a room filled with treasure: gold, silver, piles of turquoise and other precious stones worth several fortunes. Enough to tempt unscrupulous men to kill many times for it over several hundred years, beginning with Cortez. What would I do with such a treasure?" he asked, anticipating their next question. "I don't know. It's the hunting and searching for it that I love, the tracking down of clues. It's a bit of truth and history that I have to uncover. I have to know what happened to the brave men and women who gave up everything, land . . . tribe . . . home, everything important to them except integrity, in order to defend what they knew was rightfully theirs and preserve their heritage. It's a question that has burned its way into my soul, my friends, and I have made myself their personal historian."

"If it's only a legend—so far—how do you know it happened?" Chris asked. "The history books we had in school didn't mention any migration of Aztecs. Why do you believe in it, Mr. Mahler?"

"Call me Andrew, son. Everybody does."

The shadows were deepening throughout the canyon as the old prospector leaned across the railing, looking out through the wreaths of coffee steam which shivered upward in the chilly air. In his mind's eye, the flickering flames of campfires illuminated the mouths of the empty, black caves across the canyon. "I'll tell you the

14

story and let you decide from the facts what you're ready to accept." He paused, his voice taking on a timeless quality, a magic dimension of sound which held his listeners spellbound.

"When the Aztecs finally stopped here at the canyon, Cougar Canyon it has since been named because of the large number of cats that live in it, they must have been on their last legs. Traveling hundreds of miles up through unfriendly, unfamiliar terrain, they had to find food and water where they could, knowing they must never stop long enough to let their enemies catch up. They knew that to stop before they found adequate shelter and protection would mean extinction for their tribe. They had no way of knowing whether their escape had been kept a secret or whether soldiers had been ordered by an angry Cortez to track them down."

Andrew gestured out over the empty air, taking in the whole of the canyon, its distant ridges rimmed in the blue of approaching dusk. "This rocky old fort must have looked pretty good to them. It really is a kind of fort. There are plenty of caves and two back doors: the river's downstream current would push a raft out of reach of intruders in minutes, and the paths in the other direction lead out of the canyon some ten miles further on. These towering walls would protect them from surprise attack, and at the bottom, there is always an abundant supply of fresh water.

"The only apparent drawback was lack of a field for planting all the seeds they'd brought from Mexico, a place to sow and reap enough food to feed their population. The answer to that problem is what made me decide the Aztecs settled here, instead of elsewhere along the

Pecos. This is the most likely spot for a complete life-support system. You can see the place along the river where all the rock has been removed. Everywhere else, boulders and rocks are piled high. Impossible to farm. But the Indians had to create an area suitable to fill the farming needs of a sizable group of people, so they worked hard to clear a place where crops could grow. The soil along the river was apparently too sandy for their needs, so the Indians painstakingly carried down the richer soil from the plain above to deposit it in a man-made basin by the river."

They all looked down past the railing and saw that it was so. Even in the shadows, they could see that the brown color of the soil differed from the color of the sandy earth elsewhere along the riverbanks. It was soil that had probably originated above the canyon floor, somewhere in the scrub and semidesert that made up the plateau above them.

"My grandfather started at the lower end of the canyon and made his way north, exploring diligently but never finding a trace of the settlers. His love of the legend got into my father's blood, and he took up where Grandpa had left off and charted another thirty miles or so. Then I decided to look for evidence of farming. I struck pay dirt only fifteen years after I started. I've made so many maps of this canyon that it's impossible for anyone who has them to get lost. Every nook and cranny has been charted down to its last detail. Someday I'll give them to a museum or a surveying company." The pride in his voice made them realize how much he loved his work. "I've learned a lot about rocks and ore; I could tell miners where to come to mine for what they want—but

I won't—not until I find what I've been looking for. I need a lot of elbowroom."

They all smiled, thinking of the vast arena of "elbowroom" Andrew had at his disposal.

"The Aztecs had plenty of room to themselves for the first time in years and made their homes in the natural caves in this rock. They kept to themselves, and only a few prospectors and trappers and maybe some wandering Indians of other tribes ever came in contact with them. Through the years, a mystery grew up around the tribe. According to the story that people whispered about them, they took for themselves a new god. In Mexico, their most important god had been the sun, but here, living in the shadowy light of the canyon, they made another god their new, full-time protector—the fierce and deadly serpent. Rattlesnakes are common in New Mexico and Texas, and perhaps this helped them to feel secure in their new home. They became known to outsiders as the Serpent Indians, and the name stuck.

"After a while, the Indians grew careless in guarding the treasure. In their newfound security, they allowed an outsider to see what they had so carefully kept a secret from the world. And word got out. For the second time in 230 years, dishonest men began to plot to take their property from them by force."

PROLOGUE: 1750

*O*N A COLD AUTUMN NIGHT IN THE YEAR *1750, an old man stood at the mouth of a cave in the canyon, looking down at the moonlit trail beside the smoothly flowing river. He stood with the dignity of a tribal leader, and his white hair spoke of many years spent gathering the wisdom of leadership. He waited for the horde of fifty armed horsemen which his scouts had told him were already on the trail one mile away. He knew that the marauders must go slowly, both from the hazards of the rocky path along the river which they must follow to reach his tribe's domain and from the need of caution to preserve the element of surprise. He understood that the terrible threat of extinction that his people faced tonight would be as final a confrontation as the battle two hundred years before which had brought about the exodus that had led his people here. He knew that the riders who approached were driven by the same desire as Cortez and his men: the capture of a legendary treasure.*

He felt the earth abruptly shift beneath his feet. It was a normal happening in the canyon to feel earth tremble and dust fall from the walls of caves. It happened many times a year. He heard a low and powerful rumble deep beneath the rock and frowned. He had not heard this sound before, this low and angry rumble which rose

19

to shake his very soul. He made the sign of the serpent to quell the anger of the earth, but from the caves behind him came sharp screams of fear from women and children.

He listened with ears sharpened and attuned to every sound that was not native to the canyon. He could hear them now, the avaricious horsemen, only half a mile away. His warriors would not be the first to fight. Their battle weapons had grown old and dull from long disuse, and the arrows which they used to hunt small quarry in the canyon would be like toys against the well-armed horsemen they would face. Instead, they would stay silent with their families in the caves, holding quietly to that slender thread of hope which wished survival.

He heard the muffled sound of approaching hooves striking stone, and his sharp old eyes made out dark, moving shapes below him by the river. The angry earth trembled harshly at his feet, and quietly he withdrew into the shelter of the cave to wait for almost certain discovery and death.

THREE

ANDREW CONTINUED. "ONE MOONLIT night about this time of year, the treasure seekers crept stealthily through the canyon to the caves in the rock. They had taken the long, hard way to the Indian community in order to take the Indians by surprise. They had started down the riverbank many miles away, and as they drew closer to their destination, they stopped to muffle their horses' hooves with bandages of heavy cloth. The attack was well planned and would have been successful but for one fact: the Indians were no longer in their caves. The astonished thieves carefully searched every opening they could find, but there was nothing left but the warm, gray ashes of abandoned campfires. Even the pottery and cooking utensils had been left behind, full of warm, untasted food, the last supper for a vanished tribe."

"Where had they gone? They couldn't have disappeared into thin air!" exclaimed Chris, deeply interested, as usual, in a logical explanation.

Watching the excited face of his son, Tom O'Reilly remembered how he had searched each cave so carefully years before, always hoping to find a clue to the missing tribe. He felt his old interest kindle anew. The old magic of the story was still there, as spellbinding as ever.

Andrew looked speculatively at them. "Some say that the Indians prayed to their serpent-god for protection and were shown a secret way into deep, hidden caverns beneath the cliffs." He paused. "That could explain how they vanished so quickly, leaving no trail to follow, and how they avoided the well-planned ambush which cut off all paths of escape." He sat back and waited for the logical, healthy skepticism he expected from a young, intelligent mind. He wasn't long in waiting.

"There has to be another explanation," said Chris staunchly. "The Indians must have left the canyon somehow. They might have gone back to Mexico or, even more likely, to the mountains in New Mexico where there is a lot of good hunting and life is a lot easier than it must have been for them here."

Tom O'Reilly smiled and nodded at his son's quick reasoning. He had raised the same objections twenty-five years ago.

Chris continued. "The raiders were made to look foolish by the Indians, and they probably had to have some excuse for not coming back with the treasure after all their careful planning. They may have thought they were ten times more civilized and clever than any Indian tribe. When it was proved that they weren't, they refused to believe the obvious, and they blamed their failure on a serpent-god and a mysterious hole in the ground." He grinned. "It could be as simple as that."

"Okay, Andrew, tell him . . . ." Tom looked mischievously at his old friend. "How do you know there are any caverns at all if no one has ever found them?"

Andrew chuckled. "Your boy had two plausible explanations. Here's another. The Pecos River runs deep and wide through the canyon."

"Right," said two voices at once.

"This part of the canyon is mostly made of limestone, a very soft rock that is worn down by running water in a relatively short period of time; short, that is, when you consider the eons it took to form the earth as you see it now. When water penetrates limestone for hundreds and thousands of years, caves are formed down through the rock, like the Carlsbad Caverns not far from here in New Mexico. There is usually an underground river at the lowest level of the caverns. Do you see what I'm getting at?"

Chris said thoughtfully, "It could mean that if the river is a lot lower than the caves in the cliff, there could be caverns extending all the way down through the rock to the level of the river, like a giant apartment building with water in its basement. As the river sank lower and lower into the limestone over the years, new caverns would be formed all the way down." He paused. "Why do you think there's an underground river?" he asked finally. "Why should there be more than one river in this canyon?"

Andrew pointed downriver to where the cliffs curved sharply almost at right angles. The river there looked very deep, and it swirled quickly against the cliff as it curved with the rock. Above the water, they saw the dark entrances of caves.

"That wall bends out for maybe half a mile, and then it curves back in again, like a snake's back when it's crawling. It makes a bulge of rock all the way down to the level of the river and below it. This part of the canyon is laced with tunnels and caves that have been shifted and closed by moving rock even during the thirty years I've lived here. On the other side of that curve, downriver, the water behaves mysteriously. It should be a quiet pool there because it is protected by the curve of the cliff, which sends the regular river water rushing past it like the tide beyond a barrier reef in the ocean. But it doesn't do that at all. No sir. Beyond that point, the water gushes out like an uncapped oil well, underwater and considerably below the waterline. That's our underground river, taking a shortcut through solid rock as it has done for thousands of years while it was manufacturing apartment houses for Indians."

"Does it really go directly through the cliff?" asked Chris eagerly.

Andrew smiled. "Twice I sent a large piece of wood downriver through that channel, and once it traveled all the way through to the other side." He shrugged. "The second piece must have gotten caught in a dead-end cavern somewhere underwater."

No one spoke in the companionable silence of quiet excitement that men with a common interest share.

"Oh yes," continued Andrew innocently. "I left one small detail out of the story. There was a curse on the gold."

Chris looked skeptical again and Tom O'Reilly chuckled.

"It follows naturally, doesn't it, that if men had tried

and tried to capture the gold and had always failed, something must have been protecting the treasure all along? At least that's how the old prospectors figured it. They said that when someone finally does discover the gold, the serpent-god will punish him." Andrew paused and refilled his cup with fresh, black coffee. "Sometimes I think the curse came true for my father. He and I prospected these miles of canyon for years—until he disappeared."

"Like . . . the Indians?" asked Chris incredulously.

"Just as completely. It happened a long, long time ago," he said sadly, "before I met your father. My father and I had been inseparable for about twenty years, always mining and surveying together; but as he grew older, he preferred to go off by himself with his mining tools and spend the days alone. He was a careful, patient man and I never worried about him." Andrew sighed, remembering. "He never would give up the search, old and weakening as he was, and I respected him for it. It takes courage to track down a dream your whole life long and never let it go until you've realized it."

Chris watched the old miner's face and realized that although he preferred to live his life alone here in the canyon, he had never stopped missing the special companionship of his father.

"One day," said Andrew, "he took his pack and headed downriver. There had been a few earthquakes that week, more violent than usual, and he wanted to find out if the cave-ins that usually occurred had uncovered any hidden entrances. He set out to try to find a way into the caverns."

A high, light wind began to sing through the long

canyon, an eerie, lonely sound like the chanting of a great, lamenting spirit. Chris suddenly remembered that to the Indians, the wind *was* a spirit, an entity to which they prayed. He felt a strange connection with the past, as if time had never mattered here. He thought that the Indians had once sat nearby in each other's company, as he, Andrew, and his father were doing now. They must have felt the same insistent, chilling presence of the wind. As if in affirmation, its song grew louder.

Andrew seemed to hear it too. He raised his voice. "That day, I was down by the river fishing for our supper, and it didn't bother me that he took all afternoon to come back. I knew there was nothing he liked more than going off alone to excavate. That night, I cooked the fish I'd caught and set the table. After a while, the fish was cold and I went looking for him. There was no one to find. The next day and for weeks after that, I searched the canyon from end to end. I never saw him again. It seemed as it the earth had opened up and swallowed him whole. I like to believe that he found the treasure before he died. He would have wanted it that way, even if it took his life. I sometimes think that there really is a curse or whatever you want to call it—something that is protecting that gold from men who would take it, protecting it even from men like us, who seek it in a spirit of adventure and truth, as well as from the ruffians who would use it as an excuse to destroy." Andrew managed a smile. "Have I convinced you there is reason to believe in the treasure?"

Chris shivered and pulled on his jacket to shield himself from the quickening wind. "I'm beginning to hear ghost voices over there," he said half-seriously.

Andrew looked sharply at him, his deep blue eyes penetrating the boy's expression, but said nothing in answer to Chris's lighthearted attempt to return the group to a happier mood.

A deep, unpleasant laugh from the unlit cabin's open doorway shattered their composure.

FOUR

IF THE STRENGTH OF A MAN WERE TO BE measured by his size, thought Chris, then the shaggy-bearded, black-haired man before them could probably batter his way unaided through several brick walls. With at least 250 pounds of weight on a six-foot frame, he leaned casually against the doorway and smiled mockingly at Chris, revealing an uneven row of thick, white teeth. His clear and piercing eyes were as startling a blue as Andrew's and showed a sharp intelligence.

"Don't ever say you hear ghosts around here, sonny. My uncle takes such remarks much too seriously."

"Hello, Deke." Tom O'Reilly spoke so softly that his son immediately understood there was no friendship between the two men. "What are you doing here?" The tone of voice made the question seem as if a man had asked a rattlesnake why he'd left the shelter of his rock.

Deke Mahler's tan reddened noticeably. "You've aged, Tom. I wonder how you managed to climb down here after all these years." The tone was mocking.

"I wonder the same about you." Tom's voice held a hidden meaning which plainly was a private one be-

28

tween him and Deke. "There must have been a strong incentive to make you climb the cliffs again."

Deke appeared not to notice. "A family concern. I'm here to take my uncle back to the city . . . for his own good. He's too old to be living out here all alone."

Andrew's thin, clamped lips opened to growl, "I've told you fifty times, Deke, I'll never leave my home. My work is here."

"Then I'll have to change your mind, Uncle." Deke's calm was unruffled, and his confidence was vaguely alarming to Chris, who wondered if the large, subtly ominous nephew of his new friend held a trump card he could not suspect.

"As I've told my nephew," said Andrew, looking coldly at Deke, "I intend to stay here forever if need be, until I've finished my work . . . found what I've been looking for."

"What you've been looking for doesn't exist and never has existed," said his nephew. His eyes, holding that mysterious trump card in their depths again, met Andrew's confidently. His tone of voice was insulting in its placating softness, the tone a man would use to pacify a monkey. "Let's face it, you've lost your senses."

Andrew paled with rage. His cup of coffee shook gently, and he set it down with a sharp click. The thin line of his mouth clamped tight.

"Just what do you mean?" Tom asked quietly, the expression in his usually calm eyes suddenly chilling as they regarded Deke.

"Did you know my uncle can no longer distinguish fact from fiction? He's nearly eighty, you know. Old age has made him unable to think clearly anymore. Shall I go on, Uncle?" The voice was carefully solicitous, but the mocking blue eyes revealed his true enjoyment at baiting a weaker opponent.

Incredulous at the rude, uncaring way this man belittled Andrew, Chris turned to the old miner, expecting to see his wrinkled face red with anger and indignation. A shock awaited him as he stared at Andrew's pale, downcast face. The old man sat motionless, his head bowed, saying nothing.

In the silence, Deke continued with barely suppressed contempt. "Andrew has not only seen ghosts but he's heard them howl and cry as well. If he were a younger man mining for the legendary treasure in a spirit of youthful enthusiasm, this could be put down to an overactive imagination, charming and harmless. But in an *older* man," he stressed the adjective, "it shows a deterioration of the brain, and I'm afraid that if I hadn't stopped by to check on him, my uncle would have been found dead one day at the bottom of the canyon, having followed his ghosts over a cliff." He spread his hands and shrugged. "I'm here in order to prevent a tragedy."

Deke casually turned and walked to the ladder steps which descended to the slope ten feet below the deck. The bottom of the canyon was far below, but at the foot of Andrew's ladder ran a maze of pathways, some disappearing behind clumps of boulders that would dwarf even a man as large as Deke.

Deke paused at the top of the ladder. "It's a real shame my uncle will be leaving with me tomorrow. It probably means you and your son won't want to stay around for long." He looked at Tom inquiringly but found no answer in those steadily contemptuous eyes which seemed to say, "I know you too well, Deke, old friend. This situation bears some thought."

Tom O'Reilly also knew without being told that here was Andrew's reason for remaining in the canyon past the time he always traveled into town. For some reason of his own, Deke wanted Andrew out of the canyon, and the old miner was just as determined not to go.

As Deke disappeared down the trail, Andrew's head slumped lower still, and only his curling mane of snowy hair was seen, cradled in his hands.

"Ghosts, Andrew?" asked Tom with amusement tempered by a carefully concealed concern.

Slowly, the head came out of hiding and rose until Tom saw the deep blue, flashing, angry eyes of indignation, the reaction he'd been hoping for . . . a sign of life and sanity.

"My nephew isn't concerned for my health. He's after the gold." The words were spoken levelly, as a statement of fact.

"Is there any truth in what he said? Have you seen and heard strange things in the canyon?" Tom O'Reilly wasn't smiling now; his voice was serious.

"Yes." The word came flatly, as if Andrew knew how it would sound but wouldn't lie about it. His voice dropped lower. "Deke has a lot on his side, Tom. I'm afraid he'll have the power to take me away and lock me up . . . . Then he'll have the canyon to himself. I know that what I saw seems crazy, but I saw it with my own two eyes. Trouble is, I have no proof to present in a court of law in my defense."

"What is Deke's evidence?" Tom asked.

"The noises I hear at night, for a start," said Andrew tiredly.

"The sounds of Indians?" Chris asked. He felt a strong sympathy for this man who was fighting to keep the purpose in his life, the life he'd dedicated to the canyon's history years ago. Without it, he would surely shrivel up and die. A man without a purpose is a man without a reason for living, he thought, looking with new insight at Andrew's tired and troubled face. Suddenly, it didn't matter whether or not the old man's ghost experiences were real or imagined. Beside Andrew's right to life, that became a secondary issue.

Andrew looked out across the quickly darkening canyon. "Every night, a few hours after dark, the high-pitched voices start calling to each other. Sometimes they hoot and yelp just like Indians in a battle. Then I see the lights over there across the river, glowing spots of color against the cliffs. Sometimes they even move. It lasts about an hour, and afterward I can't get back to sleep. For years, there've been some sounds I never could explain. I just ignored them after a while. They're part of the canyon to me now. But these loud voices and bright lights . . . they're something new to me." The blue-black smudges beneath his sunken eyes showed he spoke the truth. "Deke has managed to make me sound like a crazy, helpless old fool with no sense at all, and he says the authorities in town will believe him, not me, take away my freedom, and lock me up in an old folks' home. He's got quite a case, hasn't he?" he asked in quiet despair.

"You've mentioned gold as his motive for getting

rid of you, Andrew. Do you mean real gold or the undiscovered treasure of the legend?" Tom asked quietly.

"I want to show you something." The old miner rose and walked inside the cabin. He was gone for several minutes, during which time they heard the agitated sound of cupboards slamming hurriedly shut as if the object of his search eluded him.

When at last he reappeared in the doorway, he was empty-handed, and his face was full of bewilderment mixed with the stirrings of further outrage. "It's gone. The serpent is gone." He sat down heavily in a rough-hewn deck chair and leaned his head back. His hand trembled as he brushed a lock of hair from his eyes. "This explains why Deke was so pleased with himself . . . so sure he'd win!" He looked at the O'Reillys without hope. "The serpent was a piece of pure gold, handcrafted by an Aztec metallurgist. It was still in perfect condition after centuries. Only this morning, I held it in my hand and admired its workmanship."

"Has Deke seen it?" Tom's voice was harsh. He saw the pattern emerging, the design to discredit every bit of evidence the old man had for establishing that he was sane.

Andrew continued in a voice exhausted from a strong emotion. "Two months ago, a week after I found it, I made a special trip to El Paso to have the serpent assayed. I was curious about its worth because I wanted a clue to the quality of the treasure. Was it pure gold or just an alloy, a mixture of gold and some baser metal? It would show me how advanced the canyon Indians had been in their craft and serve as a comparison between

33

their craft and the known work of the Aztecs. It would have given me a valuable clue to the origin of the gold. But I changed my mind. There was too great a risk that a secret this important would not be kept, and the thought of treasure hunters and gold rushers swarming all over my quiet canyon, destroying all traces of the Aztecs' history after all my years of careful, step-by-step research, turned my stomach."

"But you showed it to Deke," said Tom.

Andrew nodded. "I was so excited over my discovery that when I ran into Deke in town that day, I couldn't resist showing him the serpent. He was impressed, to put it mildly. He'd always thought the legend was foolish and untrue—the serpent changed his mind. He wanted to blast these walls apart and get the rest of the treasure out right away, but I told him I'd rather tell the world about the Aztec treasure and turn the hunt over to archeological authorities than have a rash, empty-headed person destroy all traces of their history. He didn't say much after that and we spoke of other things. He told me nastily that I looked old and tired, and I mentioned that I hadn't been sleeping well at night. I foolishly told him about strange sounds that kept me awake and that I couldn't trace. At that time, the sounds were footsteps and now and then, not often, a lonely call. He laughed and called me crazy. Then, about two weeks after our conversation, my nights became a whirlwind of noise and distraction I'd never heard before."

"Were you able to connect the new disturbances with Deke?" asked Chris.

Andrew shook his head. "I've gone over all the possibilities in my mind a thousand times a day. He may be

34

planning to destroy everything I've worked for, but I can't prove it." His voice grew hushed. "I saw strange figures in the canyon even before I told Deke about them."

The O'Reillys listened attentively.

"I've seen a huge cougar at dusk standing above me on the cliff. In all my years of living here, I've caught glimpses of big cats. They keep mostly to themselves and leave my terrain alone. But this cat is very special, almost a lion in size."

"There's nothing strange in that," said Tom reassuringly. "I've seen big cats here myself."

Andrew continued almost apologetically. "But I've seen him with a man, nearly always too distant to make out details and always at dusk, when the shadows blend all movement into indistinguishable blurs, like looking at an object underwater through a river current. I'd rub my eyes to see them better, and when I looked again, they'd be gone." He shrugged. "These sights and sounds have been part of the canyon for years and harmless to me until now." His expression darkened. "Deke's been here for five days and nights and has stood shoulder to shoulder with me when the voices cry. He's claimed to hear no sound and see no sight except the moon, the river, and the wind. He wants this canyon left alone even more than I do. He wants the rest of the treasure, and he's willing to confine me to an institution to get it. He's got me cornered—no one will believe me."

Chris attacked the problem in his mind. What they needed most was a starting point. "Tell us about the serpent, Andrew. How did you find it?"

"It was the greatest moment of my life. I was fishing

35

at my favorite place." The blue eyes had lost their indignation and sparkled now with triumph. "I looked down into the clear, blue river I was fishing in, and there it was, framed against the smooth, dark sand as if it had been put there on purpose just for me to see . . . the golden serpent of the Aztecs. I thought I was dreaming. Then I held it, dripping, in my hand and it was hard and real." The hushed tone of his voice was reverent, with the exultation of a man who has spent the best years of his life in a search that has never yielded tangible results until that moment. "I must have knelt there on the riverbank for minutes on end. I did not move. Then I looked back into the river, and suddenly, there he was, reflected from a distance in the only part of the pool that lay calm next to the shore.

"A mighty warrior, long-haired, slender, and erect with a leader's bearing, straight as an arrow like a boy. But for the first time, after all the years I had seen him from a distance, I could see the wrinkled lines of age on his thin, brown face and the wide, black eyes that never looked away. He was dressed in an animal skin and moccasins, with heavy golden ornaments worn low around his waist and a long, flat turquoise necklace shining like a universe of blue-green suns. We stared at each other through the mirror of the pool, and I was afraid to blink, afraid that if I took my eyes from his reflection and looked up at the rock on which he stood, he'd vanish in that breath of time like a ghost as he'd always done before."

Andrew paused, unaware that Tom's expression had become unnaturally attentive and that his tanned face had become paler as he listened. "Then I became aware that he wasn't alone. What I'd first taken as a large boulder at his feet became a living cat, the greatest golden cat I'd ever seen, sleek and fat, a protector of the man above him. In the next instant, raindrops shattered the reflection in the pool, and when I looked up from the distorted image in the water, the ledge was just a barren rock again. After that, a thunderstorm broke so fiercely that the river washed the canyon walls and a flash flood kept me in the cabin all day. The next morning, when I went out again to examine the ledge, I couldn't find even a paw print to prove that they'd been there. I haven't seen them since."

"Andrew . . . ." began Tom in a strained voice.

Andrew interrupted gently. "Now you know why I stayed here instead of coming into town. I can't leave Deke alone to blast his way into the historical ruins behind that cliff, ruins that belong to the world as a monument. My Aztecs deserve to have their heritage preserved intact, not blasted away into rubble by a greedy, destructive man. Those caves inside are the remnants of a courageous will to survive against desperate odds. I won't have them destroyed. It may be true that my eyes see things that aren't real," he said softly, "but if that's true, I'd rather die here than be taken prisoner by my nephew and locked up in a strange place. I don't blame you for thinking what you must be thinking. It's reasonable to doubt what you haven't seen with your own eyes. We'll discuss it further in the morning." His eyes grew cold. "Yes, I'll still be here. There's nothing Deke can do to make me leave."

The moon had risen and flooded the canyon with light. Below, the river shimmered darkly like a shiny, hunting serpent as it twisted around the base of the cliffs on its way south. The two pack animals tethered below the cabin stood closer together as the air grew colder still. Tom O'Reilly and his son looked out upon the ghostly scene and thought about the man who sat beside them and the problem that confronted him. Above the old man's tired sigh, they heard the sympathetic, lonely crying of the wind.

FIVE

TOM O'REILLY AND HIS SON WALKED cautiously through the canyon. It was dark now with the moon half-hidden behind a bank of clouds. The wind was howling between the canyon walls like ghosts on the march. They passed the river on their right. They knew the river was there only because of the muffled rushing sound on the other side of the boulders. The boulders were taller than a man, taller even than Deke Mahler, who seemed at the moment to be more than just a man. He seemed a giant in their minds, an evil giant to be fought and overcome to protect their friend.

Andrew Mahler's rights as an honest human being were in danger. Chris had never been so conscious of these rights before, rights of freedom never so simply illustrated to him as they had been this evening.

It was a powerful setting. Not only was man pitted against the elements, against the awesome canyon and the humming Pecos River, but the struggle had become man against man. And it was this type of conflict that Chris O'Reilly had never encountered before.

Chris watched his father's face, set in a stern expression. He wondered when he had met Deke Mahler for the first time and what had made them enemies instead of friends. He knew by the firm expression of his father's mouth and his unblinking eyes that whatever had happened between them had been very serious.

They made their way closer to the riverbank, using their flashlights to guide their steps. The water gently lapped against the rocks; and on small beaches here and there, it shimmered softly in the light as it approached and then receded.

Chris stopped. "Wait. I want to take a look at this." His light picked up deep, circular indentations in the water-softened sand. Paw prints. "Have you ever seen tracks this size?" he demanded. Each print was larger than his outstretched hand.

"Big cats have made the canyon their home for years," Tom replied. He pointed upward to a cave forty feet above the level of the ground and half a mile from Andrew's cabin. "We'll be well protected from wandering animals up there. That is, if some wandering animal hasn't staked his claim to it already."

"What is it?" asked Chris.

Tom smiled. "It's where I spent the nights twenty-five years ago. The caverns Andrew told you about are supposed to be behind those walls."

Chris grinned with appreciation. "It looks intact," he said, examining the pathway, narrow but secure, which led upward at an angle of thirty degrees. He put his foot upon it and felt hard, safe rock beneath. He then leaned forward, shifting his pack to the center of his back for balance. He made it to the top with only two bad moments and stood upon a small ledge outside the yawning hole.

"Don't go inside yet," warned Tom. "Make sure it's empty first."

"Come on up." Chris shined his light into the hole, half expecting to see the large, yellow eyes of a waiting mountain lion. But all he found were the cold, barren walls of a limestone cave. He heard his father approach behind him and shifted in order to make room for him to enter.

Tom stood silently at the entrance, reliving in his mind the days of long ago when he had been a young man, a little older than his son was now, and smiled, remembering. As his flashlight picked up an irregular shadow toward the back of the cave, his smile became a frown. He bent to enter and straightened up again inside as the ceiling rose to form a small cathedral dome ten feet above.

The shadow in the rear of the cave was a long, jagged crack like frozen lightning. It had been made by an earthquake, the same kind of earthquake that had shaken the canyon since history had first been recorded there. Tom carefully examined the walls for telltale weaknesses in structure. "It seems to be strong enough," he said, though frowning at the thousands of spidery lines in the rock which appeared like veins in the hands of an old, old man. "I believe we can rest here safely tonight. In the morning, we'll examine it more carefully and move to another location if we have to. But tonight," he patted the walls as if greeting an old and trusted friend, "we'll stay here."

Chris unpacked his knapsack and stacked the cans of food neatly along the walls.

Minutes later, he stood on the ledge outside, forty feet above the level of the canyon floor, and watched the moon appear beneath a massive crown of clouds to glint on the rushing waters of the river. His eyes swept the top of the cliff, where the sky made a dark blue border to the black rim of the canyon, hoping to see the dual silhouette of a man and a cat which he believed at heart to be only Andrew's imagination. Alone here, the disappointed old man, perhaps at last believing he had spent his life looking for a nonexistent tribe, could dream up legendary ghosts at will. He stopped himself reproachfully—there had been a shining element of honesty in the old miner which would prevent such daydreaming from becoming a way of life. Andrew Mahler was a man who wanted to know the truth at any cost. He wanted badly to know the history of the vanished Indians, but it was the real history he was after, not a tale of fantasy. His honest mind would accept nothing but the truth. The boy sensed, too, that the old man wanted desperately to know whether or not his sightings were hallucinations and would accept either verdict if the facts could be presented.

He turned back to the cave. "Dad . . . ." He hesitated. "Did you know Deke Mahler very well?"

Tom nodded as he shrugged off his knapsack and stretched, waiting for the question that would follow.

"What kind of man is he?" Chris watched his father's mouth become a hard, thin line.

"I don't believe my old friend Deke has changed at all. The kind of man he proved himself to be twenty-five years ago can be as dangerous now to Andrew as he was to me then."

His son was silent, waiting and sensing how important this could be to his evaluation of their large opponent.

"We both came to the canyon in the same summer. I came to look for the treasure. Andrew and my father had been friends for years, and ever since I'd heard about the legend, I'd been determined to come out here and spend some time looking for the gold. Deke didn't believe in the legend, not then at least. He came here for the challenge of it, to pit his incredible natural strength against the canyon walls and laugh at danger. He loved to climb." Tom smiled and it wasn't a friendly smile. "His body moved like a cat, muscular, lithe, and sure. He was a physical specimen of perfect health, but the wholeness of his great, capable body didn't extend to his soul. He was only physical in his relationship to life; morality didn't concern him at all."

Tom's left leg throbbed. The climb hadn't done it much good, he thought ruefully and shifted his weight onto his good leg. He leaned against the wall and looked at his son, weighing his next words carefully as if he intended to engrave them on Chris's mind forever. "Deke Mahler had a weakness, a weakness even he had not discovered. It's true. A man may have a great fear yet be unaware of it until one day it takes him by surprise. He never knows when it will happen or in what manner it will be presented, but it's a possibility that faces each and every human being. On the day when it happens, a man can be judged by his reaction to this unexpected fear."

Tom's voice grew softer, more thoughtful. "It is the way we learn about ourselves, by watching our reactions to the unexpected. And if we're disappointed in what we do that day, we have a precious chance to grow, never to make the same mistake again. Deke Mahler made a bad mistake, and he's had twenty-five years to change; but sometimes a man will stay at that same depth his spirit reached in response to the unexpected. If a man won't change himself, no length of time will do it for him. I said Deke had a fear . . . it was a fear of water."

Chris was silently attentive.

"We were climbing the cliffs together one afternoon. The sun had reached the far wall and shone down at the lowest angle it could reach before it was cut off from sight by the rocky edges of the canyon wall. The two of us were standing on the lowest ledge, looking up at the golden color of the rock, and we both saw it at the same time. What appeared to be a golden dagger, thick with jewels, was stuck in a crack above a ledge fifty feet higher. Deke was still standing there in shock when I began to climb. I reached the steep overhang, which jutted over the river, first and started up. I was a good climber, slow and sure, but I wasn't any match for Deke.

"I was thirty feet up and over the river, where one slip would send me spinning down toward the deepest water, fifteen feet or more in depth. I wasn't worried much. I'm not an excellent swimmer like you are, Chris, but I can hold my own in a peaceful pool of water. I felt Deke at my heels and paused, thinking he would speak to me. It was that pause that saved me. As I clung there, my hands holding tightly to a deep, diagonal crack in the rock, Deke's massive shoulders shoved me aside so quickly that my head struck the outcropping of rock directly above.

" 'Get out of my way!' he growled, and his eyes didn't turn to look at me as he passed. All he could see was the dagger.

"I was almost unconscious. My head felt like it was

stuffed with cotton. I couldn't see clearly, but I knew that my legs had swung out from the cliff and that the only thing that kept me from falling was the deep hold of my fingers in the fissure. In my dazed condition, if I had hit the surface of the river so far below, I would almost certainly have been knocked unconscious.

"I called Deke back just as he reached the dagger. With amazement, I watched him snarl and lift it up to throw it out ferociously into space. As it passed me, I saw that it was just a long, jagged piece of plain, hard rock shaped uncannily like a sharpened dagger. It was only the sparkle of small crystalline formations along the handle that we had mistaken for jewels.

"My grip was loosening and I cried out again. Deke looked down and for the first time in his life came face to face with his fear of water. I hung there in his line of sight, framed by the deep, blue water fifty feet below and dizzy with that bruising pain in my head from contact with the cliff, and watched Deke Mahler's face turn white.

"The fissure that held my stiffening fingers began to crumble. I tried to tell him I was going to fall. There was still time for him to reach down and give me one of those strong hands of his, still time to pull me back to safety. But I could see he didn't care. As I watched, he shivered and clung like ivy to the rock, unable to tear his eyes away from the water below. He said hoarsely, 'You're on your own, kid.' Then, with a terrible effort, he turned and began to climb straight upward, never looking back. I lost consciousness."

There seemed nothing more to say. The little cave was silent in its judgment.

At last, Tom said, "When I recovered consciousness,

I'd somehow gotten back to the cabin in spite of an injured leg."

Chris said wonderingly, "You swam out of the river and walked the half mile back and don't remember doing it? You must have had amnesia."

Tom smiled strangely. "Something like that," he said and changed the subject. "Such ruthlessness is what I've come to expect from Deke."

"So," said Chris thoughtfully, "if Deke hasn't changed in the last twenty-five years, we can expect him to do anything to get what he wants—anything at all. He'll sweep anything and anyone out of his path like he swept you off that wall." He clenched his fist as he understood for the first time the cause of his father's injured leg.

"It is a possibility we can't ignore," said Tom evenly.

An idea occurred to Chris. "If we can recover the gold serpent Deke took from Andrew, he'll know he's beaten. We'll be witnesses. He'll have to leave," he said excitedly.

Tom shook his head. "Now that Deke has had a taste of gold, he won't give up easily."

"He's a coward," said Chris contemptuously.

"Don't underestimate him, Son." Tom shook his head in warning. "We all have fears. This doesn't make us cowardly. Deke is dangerous when he's afraid because he shows a total unconcern for human life. When this occurs, watch out—the man is less than human.

"Besides," he continued slowly, "the problem of defending Andrew's sanity in court isn't the one we have to worry about. I believe Deke's approach was intended to be the easy way to get his uncle out of the canyon. It hasn't turned out that way. In fact, it's become the hardest way of all." His voice showed admiration for his old friend's stand. "Deke never intended to publicize the treasure by bringing the issue to court. Our visit has upset his plans. Andrew's more determined than ever to stay. Deke will be forced to find another way to clear the canyon. We'll have to watch him closely. He's in a corner now, afraid of being thwarted, and cornered rats are dangerous."

"But what about the lights?" insisted Chris. "There's something to Deke's story. Andrew really thinks he saw something."

Tom said nothing for a moment. Then he bent down and picked up a sandwich wrapped in foil. He tossed it over to his son. "First things first," he said. "We'll eat and grab ourselves a few hours of sleep. Then we'll explore the canyon. If anything ghostly is heard tonight, we'll be able to corroborate Andrew's story."

It was eight o'clock, and they were weary with the long descent they'd made that day. Silently, each with his own thoughts, they unwrapped their sandwiches and opened cans of warm but satisfying soft drinks.

Minutes later, Tom set the tiny alarm buzzer on his wristwatch for 10:30 and went to sleep.

Chris could not sleep. He lay upon the hard, rock floor cushioned by the softness of his sleeping bag and touched the cold limestone walls with tentative, exploring fingers. He wondered what kind of man would choose to stay alone in this harsh terrain.

He understood Andrew's reason. It was a quest, a goal to reach. It had taken strength, courage, and endurance. His admiration for the old man mounted.

47

Moments later, he fell asleep regretfully, unable any longer to forestall the delicious fatigue that came not only from the hard day's climb but from the lulling, gentle sounds of the river and the wind and the imagined whisperings of long-dead men.

SIX

CHRIS DIDN'T KNOW WHAT HAD AWAKened him. He felt uneasy as he looked groggily toward the entrance of the cave. He knew where he was and what he was doing there, but he couldn't dispel the dryness in his mouth that came from fear. He had been dreaming of an evil giant who was racing him in a contest to determine who would live or die. He could feel the giant's furnace-hot breath beat down onto his neck as he forced the muscles of his legs to run faster than they had ever run before. He felt the icy perspiration in his palms and was glad that he'd awakened when he did, but what had brought him out of the deep sleep he'd been in? He pushed himself upright and looked toward the mouth of the cave. Cold, gleaming silver ribbons of moonlight filtered in. The cave was quiet and unchanged.

He started as he heard someone release a breath of air too quickly, as if it had been held too long, and smiled sheepishly as he realized it was he.

He pulled on his shoes. The thought that something had awakened him persisted. He looked over at his

49

father's sleeping form. Tom's regular breathing told him he was sleeping peacefully.

Gradually, he became aware of something strange. He inhaled carefully. A scent of human flesh and animal skins hung familiarly on the air like heavy, natural perfume. It was a pleasant, friendly smell, but it struck fear into his mind because he knew that a visitor had come intimately close to them as they slept defenselessly and that it had been only moments ago.

He was at the mouth of the cave in a flash. The chill wind made him shiver. He kept his head down as pebbles and bits of canyon dust fell from somewhere on the cliff above. He looked up when they stopped.

The moon had frozen the night-black cavern holes onto the dead-white stone of moonlit cliffs many yards above him. It was the lifeless landscape of another planet to his unaccustomed eyes. He felt, rather than saw, the movement at the mouth of a cave, so slight that it could have been an eddy of wind; but he remembered the fall of pebbles and strained his eyes to see.

Drawn by a slight movement on a ledge nearby, Chris looked up and caught his breath. Twenty feet above him crouched a mammoth golden cougar. The filtering moonlight revealed a silkily luminous, short-haired coat which blended into the muted limestone colors in easy camouflage.

Irrelevantly, Chris remembered reading in school that the cougar was next to the largest of the American cats, second in size only to the jaguar; but looking at the immobile animal above, he sensed this was a special cat, the result of a chance mating between two giants. Another animal of this great size might not be born for a hundred years.

Before his startled gaze, so swiftly that afterwards he had to reassure himself it hadn't been imagination, it leaped and landed soundlessly at the mouth of the cave he had been watching, disappearing in a breathtaking instant of time.

Chris's expression froze at the unexpectedness of that giant leap, and then he heard the sound of voices below him, by the river.

He felt the hairs rise on the back of his neck. The sudden sweat on his body grew cold in the chill wind, making him shiver. He thought of Andrew's ghost voices. The mixed feelings of fear and a desire to know flashed through his head. All that he had learned that day, the strange presence he'd felt in the cave moments before, the sudden leap of that great cat, and now the seeming confirmation of Andrew's ghosts made his heart pound like a hammer in his chest.

The curse . . . the legendary Aztec spirits guarding the treasure from outsiders . . . could it be true? He had to know!

Chris looked quickly into the mouth of the cave where his father lay asleep. He hesitated. No, he thought, he would not wake his father yet.

From where he stood on the ledge, he could see the large, yellow square of light that was Andrew's cabin window half a mile away, and in its frame the pacing, long black shadow of a man who could not sleep. The curse . . . its mystery tortured Andrew too. Perhaps he, Chris O'Reilly, could find its source tonight and bring peace of mind to both of them. He tried to brush aside thoughts of what it might mean if he could find no logical explanation for the sounds and sights he'd heard and seen that night. The voices came again out of the dark somewhere below. He drew a deep breath and let it slowly out.

Seconds later, he was already halfway down the sloping path.

The voices had stopped by the time he reached the ground, and he hesitated, not knowing which way to go. A group of boulders, ten feet high and taller, sat at the river's edge some yards away like giant prehistoric mushrooms. He started toward them uncertainly as his eyes grew able to distinguish objects in his path and shapes became dark gray against the black of shadow.

Lost among the boulders, he clearly saw the pale, majestic cliffs above him lit by the moon, which had completely left its cloud cover and shone down with a clear brilliance. That was better than a lantern, for it threw the rugged geography of the canyon into sharp relief.

Hesitantly, he surveyed the landscape and noticed a small clearing by the river, not far away. It lay directly opposite the cabin.

The moon caught a reflecting surface there. He started toward it as he realized it was not the water but a round object about a foot in diameter, unmistakably man-made.

As he walked toward it, Chris stumbled across a bulky object on the ground which was so heavy that it didn't yield as his foot hooked it. He fell and hurt his leg.

Sitting up with a groan, he rubbed the bruise which

was already forming on his calf and grimaced as he stood up.

He bent down to examine the dark object, hooding his light with his hand. "It's a battery," he said thoughtfully to himself, "a twelve-volt portable."

The shiny surface of the reflector caught his eye again, and when he picked it up, he knew what it was for. He knew without even thinking. It was a searchlight, a foot in diameter and powerful, powerful enough to cast moving spheres of light on the tall, silent cliffs above him across the river. The same moving lights that had convinced Andrew he was seeing some manifestation of the Aztec tribe and had given Deke Mahler the excuse to charge Andrew with senility.

A flood of relief washed over him. So there *was* a logical explanation for the lights that Andrew saw! With the relief came anger. No long-dead Indian tribe was responsible for this. Deke was. He knew this as surely as he knew what Deke was after. The gold. The treasure he would do anything to get.

In the midst of his relief, one part of his mind thought of the great golden cougar he had just seen. It was the animal which, in Andrew's experience, usually accompanied an Aztec chieftain. Had he dreamt it? It had happened so fast. He frowned. It didn't fit this man-made performance staged by Deke. He would think about that later.

Chris said aloud in a voice edged with contempt, "There were voices too." He whirled around and looked among the rocks. He found it at once. A recorder. It was an instrument that almost certainly would have ghost voices upon it: howling, eerie voices which would drive an ordinary man insane with incomprehension but which, as yet, had given Andrew only food for thought. Beside the mechanism sat two opened crates. The lettering on their sides read DYNAMITE. Another, smaller box was nearby, full of flares. One way or another, Deke was determined to break in and get the gold.

With quick, angry movements, Chris disconnected the searchlight from the battery. He grasped the handle of the small recorder and jerked the machine away from its amplifiers, snapping the connecting wires. He would take them back to the cave to show his father. Then, together, they would take them to Andrew's cabin. Deke Mahler was in for a surprise!

He stared up at the still-lit cabin with undisguised anger. Somehow, he thought with determination, he and his father had to stop this contemptible charade. They couldn't let Andrew's nephew get away with what he planned. He stood silently, his ears alert to any sound above the river and the wind. There must be another crook around to run the machinery while Deke plays his little game, he thought grimly. The voices he'd heard had not been the Indian calls that Andrew had described. They must have been Deke and someone else discussing what to do now that he and his father had come to the canyon. He felt sure of it!

He carefully scanned the moonlit path that wove in and out among the boulders uphill toward the cabin and saw no one upon it.

Then he looked up at Andrew's cabin and stiffened to attention. Two human shapes were visible in the cabin window. One of them, recognizable by size alone, was unmistakably Deke Mahler.

Another thought struck Chris, and he stood silently reasoning it out. Andrew! Tonight he'd be expecting to hear the Indian calls as usual. For the first time in weeks, he would be disappointed. Deke would probably have told his confederate not to operate the lights and recorder tonight because the O'Reillys were in the canyon.

Chris knew the old man's mind was already under strain. When he saw and heard nothing tonight, what would he think? Would he doubt his own sanity as Deke wanted? Or would the real reason for the ghosts' silence, tonight of all nights, occur to him?

Chris cast a swift glance downriver toward his father's cave and made a quick decision. His father could take care of himself; he faced no present danger, and the alarm would awaken him within the hour. But Andrew might need help any minute now.

He headed quickly toward the cabin, checking each curve along the boulder-lined path for any trace of Deke's unknown companion, but he saw no one and arrived safely at the foot of the steep stairs that led up to Andrew's deck.

The large front room was still alive with light, and Chris heard voices, muffled by the walls. He strained his ears to hear, but the words were indistinguishable.

The front door opened and closed with a bang. Involuntarily, Chris stepped into the darker shadow of a rock. He saw Andrew lean over the railing and his old eyes peer intently at the wall across the river. The black holes of caves in the rock remained cold and black and still. He cocked his head and listened.

"Nothing!" Andrew muttered. "Why tonight when my friends are in the canyon and can prove me right?"

"Andrew," Chris whispered as loudly as he could, "I found a searchlight and recorder."

The screen door opened more slowly this time and closed softly. The large, dark bulk of Deke Mahler quietly approached.

"Why tonight?" demanded Andrew, but there was a new confidence in his tone. "Where are the voices and lights tonight?"

"What voices and lights?" Deke's voice was as smooth as ever, with a hint of derision now coloring his insulting words.

Andrew seemed not to have heard. "There's something strange about the absence of those lights, Nephew. I've heard them louder every night since I told you about the gold . . . much louder than before I told you I was hearing things!" He looked intently out into the canyon, but the watching boy knew that he was giving himself time to think.

Suddenly Andrew's fist slammed down on the wooden railing, making the old wood quiver. "Now I have it!" He whipped around to face his nephew. "You wanted me to see those lights so that you could deny they existed, to make me doubt my own sanity and leave the canyon. You must have some kind of apparatus that produces those lights and sounds and a friend to run it for you. You want me out of the way so badly that I'd put nothing past you. But I'm not going, Deke. I'm staying, and when I tell my friends what you've done, they'll act as witnesses on my behalf in a court of law. I'll bring the suit myself . . . against you and your dishonest friend!" he said with angry contempt. Chris winced, hearing the brave words and knowing that the old man was leaving his criminal relative with no alternative but force.

Deke Mahler was silent, and Chris watched his moonlit face, nasty with rage as he felt himself challenged by his uncle, a stubborn old man whose strength was no match for his, who hadn't given up in the face of carefully planted evidence that he had lost his reason and now stood firm, confronted by the superior physical force of a younger, stronger man. It was an unexpected obstacle that caught Deke by surprise. This pointless opposition made him want to break things. His large hands clenched into fists at his sides.

Then, with a short, ugly laugh, Deke ground out his cigar on the wooden railing and flung it into the dark. It landed with a soft hiss at Chris's feet, but Deke's angry gaze hadn't bothered to follow its flight, and the boy relaxed. "Don't worry, old man. Those sounds and sights will never bother you again. In fact," he looked at his watch, "in just about three minutes, all our worries will be over."

Chris looked at his watch. Three minutes until 10:00, a full half hour before his father was due to be awakened by the buzzer on his watch. He listened, puzzled. A sudden connection in his mind made him catch his breath. The voices below their cave—those boxes of dynamite he'd seen beside the light and recorder—the fact that the cave was just forty feet above the bend in the river that held the secret of the hidden treasure. His hands grew cold and icy with his anticipation of Deke's next words.

"All our worries?" asked Andrew, puzzled, his thoughts momentarily on another track.

"Your lights, my gold, the O'Reillys' interference." Deke grinned, and the moonlight showed his jagged, irregular teeth at their ugliest, the teeth of a carnivore, a barracuda. "I'm about to dispose of all our birds with one stone."

Chris groaned. Running the distance back to the cave in three minutes was almost an impossible feat, but he had to make the effort. He dropped the searchlight and recorder and turned to run but hit the muscular hardness of a human rock. Two arms the size of well-fed boa constrictors seized and held him with slight effort, and the long, rectangular face which looked down at him was frightening in its lack of intelligence. He saw a second man nearby. He felt himself pushed backward in the direction of the steps.

"What's that?" faltered Andrew as he leaned over the railing and saw who was below. "Who are those men, Deke, and what are they doing with the boy?"

Deke turned to look. His expression darkened and he cursed aloud. "Sully," he said between clenched teeth to the smaller man, "I told you two to keep an eye on that cave! Where's his father?"

"The kid came out alone, Boss," the man called Sully answered. "We followed him."

"Didn't I tell you to make sure they didn't leave that cave?"

"Aw, Boss, we didn't have a chance to set the charges like you told us to. Something woke him up." The little man grabbed Chris's arms and jerked them up his back. "You can let go now, Dutch. I've got him."

Chris looked at the two men who held him captive. They were as unalike as night and day. Sully, the one who stood behind him holding his wrists in a viselike grip, was the ugliest human being he'd ever seen. The creature had wide-set, slitted eyes, a pug nose, and a wide, thin mouth. His sneering face looked as if a great weight had slowly compressed his skull during his formative years, leaving this grotesquely flattened image. The long, thin, lashless eyes were evil with enjoyment as the small, ugly man twisted Chris's wrists further up his back, more, it seemed, to cause him discomfort than to immobilize him. The man was far below average height but somehow exhibited a strength unknown to normal men, a strength that came from a maladjusted mind, a mind adjusted to shameful ends.

The man called Dutch, a taller, stronger man who stood near Sully, exhibited the dull expression of a man of subnormal intelligence. A giant who dwarfed even Deke Mahler, Dutch stood quietly nearby, like a machine at rest. His large, round eyes seldom blinked. Looking at him, Chris felt certain that he merely took orders without thought or question. His shoulders hurt where the large hands had grasped him. Despite the circumstances, he felt an overwhelming relief that Deke's plans had gone awry.

"You were planning to dynamite Tom O'Reilly and his son in that cave?" Andrew's face was pale and old and suddenly full of fear, fear of the inhuman mind he now knew he was dealing with.

"Never mind." Deke's expression had returned from disappointed anger to his usual self-confidence. "We've got all night before us and two extra hands to help. With two boxes of explosive and flares for light, we'll have that gold by morning."

"You'll never have the gold!" croaked Andrew. His words came slowly but with the force of water shooting through a tiny crack in the world's largest dam. "Those cliffs are too thick to blast through if you don't know what you're doing. I've mapped them. I know what it will take to enter them. If you harm Tom or his son, you can set those charges night and day for weeks and never find the right combination." Andrew turned to go and was stopped by Deke's large hand.

"You're awfully confident, old man. You don't hold any cards now. I know where your maps are."

There was satisfaction in Andrew's voice when he answered. "Do you think you're the only one who can plan? When I discovered you'd taken the gold serpent, I took my maps out of their drawer." He smiled coldly and gestured at the canyon. "They're hidden where you'll never find them."

Deke's face flushed dark with violent anger. His large, hairy hand rose and swept across the old man's face in a painful slap. The harsh sound sped through the canyon and was immediately displaced by the short, confident laugh that came from Andrew's bleeding mouth.

"Let the boy go," Andrew ordered. "If you harm him, nothing you will ever do for or against me will get you through those cliffs to the gold. I'm in a position to bargain now. Our lives for the treasure. And the bargain starts with Tom O'Reilly's life. Otherwise, you'll never see the maps again."

Deke paused as if to consider all the possibilities, but they knew he had only one to choose. "All right, old man. Your friends for your maps. Hand them over."

Andrew shook his head. "Not until I see Tom."

Deke smiled dangerously. "Sully, you and Dutch go get him. Make sure you don't lose him."

"We're going with you," said Chris boldly, unwilling to let these strange, rough men harm his father. He winced as his wrists came higher up his back. "Is it necessary for you to break my arms?" he demanded.

"Okay, Sully, you can let him go now."

"Aw, gee."

Chris's hands were suddenly freed, and the boy eased them down his back. He turned around to look down at the little man who had caused him so much discomfort. As their eyes met, Chris shivered. This man enjoyed his work. He would be careful not to get in his way more often than was necessary. Somehow he felt that it would be necessary in the very near future. Next go-round, he vowed he'd pick the time and place.

"Why not?" mused Deke. "Why don't we all take a little stroll to the cave."

Chris felt uneasy. Deke was reacting too calmly to Andrew's trump card. He felt certain that Deke had no intention of bargaining with his uncle for the maps and that he had already formed a plan to get them anyway.

SEVEN

The wind rose as they neared the river and covered the sound of their footsteps. The moon was still as bright as ever, and although Deke carried flares, he made no move to light them. He intended to catch Tom O'Reilly off guard.

Chris looked up at the mouth of the cave as they stopped at the foot of the cliff. Even if his father should awaken now, he thought helplessly, there was nothing he could do. If Tom should resist, Deke would threaten the welfare of his son and his friend, and Chris knew that his father would never allow concern for his own safety to cause harm to another human being if he was able to prevent it. He would surrender to the gang and Deke would have them all.

Beneath the shelter of the overhanging rock, Deke lit a flare. It sputtered to life.

Chris placed his foot upon the sloping ledge that led up to the cave's mouth. A large hand on his shoulder held him back. He didn't have to look behind him to know that it was Deke. He turned back angrily and looked into Deke's grinning face.

Deke signaled to Sully, who walked straight to the cliff wall directly beneath Tom's cave. In a hole in the rock there, he set two sticks of dynamite. Quickly, he unrolled a long, white fuse and let it out for several feet. Then he deftly attached it to the fat, deadly sticks. He fished in his pocket, found a book of crumpled matches, and tore one off. Kneeling beside the fuse, he held it up for all to see and waited, grinning, for an order from Deke.

Chris wanted to cry out, but he was afraid he might bring his father to the mouth of the cave at the moment of the explosion.

Deke turned to Andrew, who instantly knew the part he was to play.

"The maps," Andrew said tonelessly, looking up at the silent mouth of the cave where Tom O'Reilly slept. "His life for the maps, is that it?"

"You got it," drawled Deke.

At his nod, Sully struck the match. It flickered and danced before their eyes, cupped in the palm of his hand.

"Sully's getting tired of holding that heavy match all by himself, aren't you, Sully?" said Deke, his hand still on Chris's shoulder. He grinned as the boy's muscles grew tense with anger.

The ugly little man guffawed. The match was halfway burnt. "I sure don't want to burn my fingers, Boss. If it gets down too much farther, I guess I'll just have to let it drop onto the fuse."

"The maps are in my stove, behind the wood," said Andrew roughly.

"Really?" said Deke casually. "What a careless place to put them. I don't think I believe you." His eyes flickered over to Sully, whose short, ugly form looked evil in the pulsating light of the flare which hissed nearby. Shadows, light and dark, danced quickly on the cliff face, dying before the light could fully illuminate the cave where Tom O'Reilly slept.

"It's true!" Andrew pushed forward toward Sully but was stopped by Dutch, who just reached out and hooked a finger through his arm. "I wouldn't let you light the fire tonight, remember? You wanted to, but I told you we were out of wood. I needed time to put them somewhere safer, but you never left me alone."

"That's true," mused Deke. "All right, old man, I believe you. Light it, Sully."

While Andrew and Chris watched in horror, rooted to the spot by the unexpectedness of Deke's vicious command, Sully released the still-glowing match. It fell soundlessly on the fuse and ignited it.

"No!" roared Chris as he lurched toward the spark that crept too quickly, hissing like a snake, in the direction of the explosive.

Dutch had been waiting for such a move. Easily, with one hand, his other hand still gripping Andrew, the giant pulled the fighting boy back toward the shelter of a pile of head-high boulders fifty feet away. In the space of seconds, they were all safely protected. Chris lay flat on his stomach, held in place by the enormous, unmovable weight of Dutch. His mouth was bitter with the taste of sand.

"Tom never could be trusted to mind his own business," murmured Deke, his eyes alight with satisfaction. "Now he won't mess up my plans."

As his words ended, a thunderous noise blotted out

all other canyon sounds. A storm of dust and stinging rocks hailed around their heads for what seemed like minutes. Then there was only silence and the singing of the river and the wind.

Deke lit another flare. He held it up and stepped around the boulder to look up at the cave. Chris and Andrew, quiet now, followed him.

A huge pile of rubble, blown down by the explosion, lay at the foot of the cliff, and the settling of loose rock made a rattling sound. The entrance of the cave had widened to triple its former size, and its mouth drooped down, forming a bulging ledge which had not been there before. Thick, jagged cracks like frozen lightning shot up the cliff wall.

"Not bad for a first try, eh, Sully?" said Deke as he surveyed the damage with satisfaction. "We'll just have to set a bigger charge next time when we have those maps to find the proper place to blast."

"The pack of you are murderers and thieves!" cried Andrew hoarsely, his eyes on the cave forty feet above. The light cast upon the opening showed dust still billowing in heavy, white clouds from the cave's mouth.

Before anyone could guess his intention or move to stop him, Chris leaped to the settling pile of rocks and scrambled over it in stumbling steps. He climbed steadily up to where the broken ledge hung into space and was on the path in seconds.

When he entered the torn-out mouth of the cave moments later, it was an alien place. The surface of the rock walls, which had been cracked with myriads of tiny veins, had fallen onto the cave floor, widening the space between the walls and hollowing out a new and larger cave. A long, jagged opening in the floor had burst out-ward like a fissure in an overripe tomato, leaving a crevasse large enough to swallow a man. It lay directly beneath the spot where Tom O'Reilly had been sleeping.

Head-high mounds of cracked and settling rock lay behind the crevasse and all around it. There was no sign of life. Tins of food had fallen from their neatly stacked positions on the wall where Chris had set them earlier. Some of them lay partway down the crevasse, their bright labels plainly visible in the glare from the small flash-light Chris had unhooked from his belt.

The boy looked at the hole in mounting horror. He shined the light down into the long, white crack, but the beam diffused before it reached the bottom, leaving the crevasse unexplored and of mysterious depth.

There was no sign of his father.

He heard the approach of climbers from below but paid scant attention. The vertical shaft before him was large enough to accommodate a man the size of Deke Mahler and certainly large enough to engulf the falling form of Tom O'Reilly, made awkward and helpless by sleep.

Suddenly, the ground shifted again beneath his feet. Pieces of rock fell into the hole with little thuds and bounced and rattled their way down until the sound became so faint it disappeared.

As the earth moved before his eyes, partially closing the crevasse, the boy felt dizzy and sick, not only with the shift in equilibrium but with the certain knowledge that his father was trapped helplessly below. His fears were confirmed as his flashlight settled on a pair of climbing boots which lay against the far wall of the cave where Tom O'Reilly had unlaced them. He began to lower himself carefully into the hole and was stopped by a heavy hand on his shoulder.

"No you don't," said Deke Mahler. Andrew, Sully, and Dutch entered the cave behind him. "Nobody climbs down that shaft tonight. If Tom's down there, that's his bad luck. I need you out here to help me find that gold."

Stepping from the hole, Chris felt a violent, terrible anger. Without warning and with all the strength his one hundred sixty-five pounds could summon, he lunged toward Deke, catching him completely by surprise as he stood confidently above him, the curious faces of Sully and Dutch visible on either side of Deke's big body. The force of the impact sent Deke reeling toward the cave entrance, his massive arms knocking Andrew aside and the other two men back as easily as if they had been feathers in the wind.

Andrew's head hit a rock, and the force of the blow knocked him out.

With a grunt of surprise, Deke flailed his arms backward and, like his cohorts, disappeared from sight as he fell ten feet to a wide, flat ledge, a lucky breaking point for a fall that would have carried him to the sharp edges of pointed rock forty feet below.

Angry voices came from just below the cave.

"I'll fix that kid!" yelled Sully.

Chris heard the sound of climbing coming closer. He knelt again at the hole where he thought his father had fallen. Just then, he felt a hand on his shoulder. He whirled around, ready to fight again. His anger turned to shock.

"Dad!" he choked. He grasped his father's arm as if

he wanted to reassure himself Tom was really there and not down the hole after all.

Tom glanced swiftly at the cave entrance. He pulled Chris quickly back behind a pile of fallen rock at the rear of the cave. He put his finger to his lips and shook his head in warning.

"But Andrew!" whispered Chris urgently.

Tom shook his head again.

The man and boy crouched behind the rock and watched and listened. No sooner had they concealed themselves than they saw Deke Mahler climb through the entrance. "Where's that kid!" he snarled, looking around fiercely.

From their hiding place, they saw Andrew lying quietly against the wall where he'd been thrown during the brief scuffle. As they watched, he stood up shakily and tenderly touched a large, swelling bruise on his forehead. At Deke's angry words, he glanced around him at the empty cave in shocked bewilderment. He stepped to the crevasse and leaned over it, peering into the darkness.

"Tom? Chris?" Andrew called urgently. A few pebbles dislodged by his boot rolled down into the shaft and were his only answer. He looked tired and defeated, a bent old man who all at once had seen too much of the ugly side of life.

Suddenly, without warning, Andrew was thrown against the wall. No one was close enough to have hurled him with such force. An earth tremor had been triggered by the blast. A low rumble in the rock below grew louder and louder, and limestone dust floated heavily throughout the cave. Andrew lay still against the wall, pinned by the unstoppable geological force of rock moved by unknown, inestimable pressures. Before his horror-stricken eyes, the crevasse relentlessly crumbled inward. In seconds, it was over, leaving a pile of crushed and crumbling rubble on the floor, a sealed and certain tomb, Andrew thought, for Tom and Chris.

With a scream, he flung himself upon the debris, clawing it away with his fingers. On his knees, he worked desperately to free the crevasse from the heavy rock which packed it.

Deke too had fallen to the floor. He sat there, dazed. Sully and Dutch climbed through the mouth of the cave, and the giant helped Deke to his feet.

"What was that, Boss? And what happened to that kid?" asked Sully in puzzlement.

"They're down there, both of them," Andrew cried helplessly. "The earthquake sealed them in!"

"Come on, old man," said Deke. "We're going to find that gold tonight."

"I'm not coming!" whispered Andrew hoarsely.

Deke stood over his uncle for several moments, and then a smile of contemptible unconcern made his face as unpleasant as a human face could be. "Get on your feet," he commanded. "We're going to get those maps."

"You've got to help me clear the hole!" pleaded Andrew. "They're trapped inside! Maybe they're still alive!" Tears of helpless outrage streaked his dusty face as he turned toward his nephew.

Strong hands lifted him from the floor. There was no way he could stop them now. Deke had the upper hand. There was nothing he could do to help his friends.

Gradually, a look of calmness replaced the desperation in Andrew's face. He hid this expression from Deke and lowered his head until it was in shadow. The look on his face told the watching O'Reillys that Andrew believed they were dead and meant to make his nephew pay for their deaths. He didn't know yet how he'd do it, but he was certain of one thing: he'd find a way.

PROLOGUE: 1760

*I*N A CAVERN DEEP BENEATH A HUNDRED
*tons of rock, the tribal architect surveyed the finished
rooms with pride. He thought of his tribe's history, filled
with violence that had necessitated flight from the cov-
etous, greedy men who sought the treasure. He thought
of the initial indignation of his peaceful people which
had become an angry fear, the constant fear of conquest
and betrayal, even now while safely hidden in the caverns underground.*

*He looked around him at the eternal inhabitants of
the burial chamber. They lay at rest along carved ledges
in the wall, the dead men and women of his tribe. They
numbered forty-five, a greater number now by half than
those who lived within the dwelling chambers in other
parts of the caverns. His was a dying tribe, but now they
had a legacy, eternally untouchable, a fitting tombstone
for a once-great nation. He met the hollow stares of the
dead with fierce compassion. If their angry spirits failed
to stop the trespassers when they came, there were other
dangers in the rooms ahead. His glance rested on the de-
cayed form of a man in ceremonial clothing, who sat
propped like a judge in a seat against the lower step of
the entrance to the treasure room.*

*It was the old man who had first led his people to
the safety of the hidden caverns ten years before. He had*

spent his last productive years devising a foolproof way to prevent evil men from ever being successful at their thievery. The architect could still see the drawn, wrinkled face of his white-haired leader as he lay upon his bed awaiting death. The old eyes had sparkled with the fire of satisfaction at having solved a mighty problem. "You will build a place to house our treasure, a place hidden from all outsiders. This is the design." The shaking fingers had held out to him a scroll of dried animal skin filled with drawings. It was a plan for protecting the treasure long after the last members of the tribe had turned to dust, no longer able to act as guardians for the legacy they owned.

"The gold belongs to us alone and we will keep it!" The passionate promise of the architect's dead leader echoed in his mind as he watched his workers gather their tools and leave. He smiled, knowing that five years of expert craftsmanship at strategic places in every tunnel and cavern had achieved to perfection the old man's plan. From this day on, no stranger would ever see the treasure and survive.

EIGHT

THE SOUNDS OF THE DESCENT OF DEKE and his companions grew fainter, leaving the torn mouth of the cave quiet and dark. Only the feeble light from a dying flare abandoned on the ledge outside shone through.

Then from behind the mounds of cracked and sifting rubble at the back of the cave appeared two serious faces, warily looking out to make certain they were alone.

"They're gone, Dad," said Chris grimly.

"Watch your step," Tom O'Reilly cautioned in a low voice. As he came forward into the light, the marks and scrapes along his face and neck showed how close his escape from the explosive's force had been. Beneath his feet, he felt the echo of a tremor, a very slight movement of the earth, an indication of what might come or might have passed already. "It wouldn't take much to bring the ceiling down upon our heads."

They crept toward the entrance and looked down.

On the ground below, another two flares had been lit and sputtered away, revealing a small, hunched figure in their glow. Sully hovered busily over a box of dynamite, sorting out the sticks and wrapping them in bundles with their fuses.

On the path to the cabin now, the movements of three figures were seen by the light of a flare held aloft by the upraised arm of Dutch.

Tom located his shoes and sat down to put them on.

"I wish we could have told Andrew where we'd really gone," said Chris with concern. "I'll bet he feels more alone than anyone in the world."

"I know," said his father softly. "But it was the genuineness of his grief that convinced Deke we'd been buried in that crevasse. It would have taken only one false expression to make him smell a rat and start looking around. It's given us one big advantage. Everyone believes we're dead. We're the last people on earth they'll expect to see again. This leaves us free to work toward helping Andrew, for you can be certain they know they can't afford to let him live to tell about Deke's treachery. It's up to us to stop them."

"How?" asked Chris helplessly. "There's no way down from here without being seen. We'd never make it; Sully'd see to that. And if we stay here, the first explosion Deke sets off will bury us for real. How can we stop them now?"

Tom laughed softly. "By meeting Deke in the place he'll least expect to find us. By taking the path I searched for when I was a boy, the path that Andrew has searched all his life to find. A shortcut to the Aztec treasure." He rose and moved to the rubble at the rear of the cave where they had crouched, hiding from Deke. "I saw it while I lay here catching my breath after the blast." He unhooked a small flashlight from his belt and cupped it in his hand to reduce the yellow light to a reddish glow.

In its subtle light they saw the opening of a tunnel, a darker black against the black of shadowed walls. The focused beam fell upon the rock above the tunnel entrance. The light revealed a strange carving set deep into the wall, head-high above them. A most frightening image, so sinister and realistic that it seemed to have been carved as a warning to those who might enter.

The figure was a serpent. They stood in silence, regarding the almost hypnotic image. The massive head and body of the creature stood out from the wall in an unusually convincing pose. It seemed to be alive in its poised readiness to strike. Whoever had carved it had been a master of his craft.

They stared at it, spellbound.

"The Aztecs' symbol!" breathed Chris in awe. His foot kicked aside a few loose rocks at the entrance, and he squatted down to peer into a dark hole that led off horizontally into the rock, appearing to be high and wide enough for human passage. He grabbed the side of the entrance with his one free hand and shined his light inside. The blackness of the hole ahead showed dust as thick as that in their cave.

They felt the earth shift again beneath their feet. Clouds of dust from limestone particles, airborne as the broken cave rock settled, filtered through the air, making them choke and cough.

They quickly searched the cave. The cave-in had buried all their equipment. Their only means of survival lay in what they carried with them. Flashlights and pocket knives.

Tom stepped inside the tunnel with Chris close behind. The passage ahead widened sufficiently for the two to walk upright and abreast. The way was clear of rubble, and in ten minutes they were deep inside the rock. The cave had been forty feet above the canyon floor; but their gently sloping path had led downwards, and now they were an unknown distance above the level of the river, with no compass to tell them in what direction they were traveling and only the earth's gravity to tell them which way was up or down.

They walked quickly, guided by the steady, bright beam of Tom's flashlight. Soon they came to a fork. One narrow path led upward; the other led downward, a gradual slope that turned a corner and disappeared from sight.

"We'll try the upper tunnel first," said Tom hoarsely, still choking from the dust that fell continuously as the sound of their feet reverberated off the walls of the long-abandoned passageway.

They turned left and began a slow ascent, but before they had gone very far, they came to a dead end. It was a certain dead end, for the place through which the tunnel must have led before was packed with solid rock, the result of other earthquakes of perhaps many years before. It was hopeless even to think of digging out past these crushing tons of rock in the short time they had left. Already, the air was thickening, making their lungs work harder to glean fresh, life-giving oxygen. The rock had solidified with the passage of time and the tremendous weight of the cliffs above. If the thought of moving that rock bare-handed entered their minds, they quickly rejected it. Machinery, skill, and knowledge of the dangerous geological pressures of packed and shifting rock would be necessary now to clear that tunnel.

They returned to the fork, knowing that their only path now lay in the gentle, downward curve of passage which began there. They also knew that if this did not work out, they would have to return to the cave from which they'd started and chance discovery by a cruel and crafty Sully on their climb back down the cliff.

At the fork, they left the upward tunnel and entered the downward sloping passageway, walking slowly but purposefully toward the curve which partially hid the descent. They stopped dead as they rounded it, confronted by another cave-in.

"I guess we'll have to go back," said Chris sadly.

"Not until I see how bad this rockfall is," Tom answered with determination. "Hold your light on the pile." He laid down his own flashlight, loosened the buttons of his jacket sleeves, and bent down for the first large, jagged piece of rock.

They felt as much as heard the vast explosion. When the vibrations from the blast reached them, they were sent tumbling back against the walls.

"They've started," whispered Chris. His horrified gaze turned as they heard the breaking up of rock only yards away at the tunnel's fork. Heavy thuds jarred the tunnel floor. The air grew thicker with dust.

Tom reached down, grabbed his flashlight, and centered it on a solid wall of rock that had not been there before, a blockage that cut off the fork and their only path to the outside.

The O'Reillys lay paralyzed with the sight and the realization that the tunnel air, never fresh, was growing fouler by the minute.

We're trapped. There's no way out, thought Chris silently. He began to shiver, imagining that the rock was closing in around him. He felt the receding tremors of the earth beneath his feet.

His father had said that someday each man would have to face a hidden fear, a fear that would prove him a man or less. It had happened to Deke Mahler; now it was happening to Chris O'Reilly. A fear of suffocation clutched his chest as if it were a vise squeezing all the air from his lungs. To his panic-stricken mind, the walls seemed to be moving closer relentlessly, and he threw out his shaking arms to keep the walls apart. At the touch of the cold, hard stone, he felt the distant tremble of a passing earthquake and moaned with fear. At least, he thought hysterically, Mahler was still alive twenty-five years after his confrontation. Then he caught his shaking breath and consciously controlled his panic-driven breathing to bring it back to normal. With a determined effort, he succeeded. He smiled grimly. Claustrophobia had squeezed his mind like a vise, bruising his thinking, normally clear and strong. Would he really choose to live an extra quarter of a century as a Deke Mahler? Almost his old self again, he shrugged off the vise.

Tom turned to look at him and put his arm around his son's shoulders.

Chris smiled at him, and there was no longer any sign of the hopelessness and despair that had threatened to cut him off from the life-or-death dilemma that confronted him.

He stood silently for a moment, comparing the two piles of rock. "Well," he said at last, turning back to the older cave-in, "this one's filled with smaller rocks. We should be able to move them faster. Maybe it's shallower, too." He bent down for the first rock, knowing that, shallower or not, they had to make the effort.

For half an hour, they worked steadily with strong hands to lift rocks and pocket knives to widen cracks for leverage, an occasional cough or gasp the only sound besides the clink and clunk of rock on rock. With flashlights wedged into clefts in the walls beside them, they reduced the mound of rock before them. The tunnel behind them began to look like the crumbled wall of a crusader's castle after a siege of months.

As the rock pile mounted, the air became progressively fouler. They panted from the exertion and the bad air which they were forced to breathe.

They stopped as seldom as they could and only when it was necessary to stop the choking in their throats, which they could briefly do by bowing their heads momentarily and breathing through a handkerchief.

Slowly, the cave-in was diminished.

Chris was working steadily, ignoring the sweat that made his clothing uncomfortably clammy in the cold tunnel, when all at once he stopped. The stone that he had just pried loose fell out of his hands and rolled away, unnoticed.

"Don't move that light!" he whispered hoarsely. With trembling hands, he scraped away the dust.

A human shoe designed for a white man, not an Indian, lay before him, almost white with limestone dust. The rotting laces had been broken many times and re-tied with great care into small, perfect knots, the work of a patient, frugal man. The sole was worn down at the heel as if it had been used to walking many miles a day. Through a hole in the worn toe, there was a gleam of white.

Chris felt further and recoiled involuntarily as his fingers touched a smooth, cold surface, jagged and broken along the thinness of its length.

"Bring the light closer," he murmured tonelessly to his father, already knowing what it was.

Light hit the shoe and illuminated it harshly against the irregular shadows of the piles of stone that lay around it. Quietly encased in its rotted leather was the tibia of a human leg, splintered and broken beyond repair. It had been an injury great enough to kill through shock alone in a matter of moments.

"He's been here for a long, long time," Chris said in a strange, low voice.

Mechanically, he lifted the rest of the rock from the human remains beneath. The skeleton lay lengthwise among bits of rotted clothing. Underneath the rock beside it, they found a pickaxe.

They looked at one another in understanding and agreement.

"Andrew's father," said Tom quietly. "It's Andrew's father."

"He must have discovered a secret entrance somewhere in the cliffs outside," whispered Chris. "Poor Mr. Mahler. He thought he'd found his treasure and climbed down here, only to be trapped when the earth shifted."

Tom looked down at the splintered leg. "At least he didn't suffer."

They became painfully aware of the stifling atmosphere of the close-walled tunnel and resumed their rock-moving in silence, watched by the hollow eyes of the old prospector's skeleton as it lay against the wall upon its back. They worked feverishly now to clear away the rest of the fallen rock. The pile was noticeably diminishing, for they could see a chink of deep black beyond the cave-in. Even when they had enlarged the hole, shining the torch through it provided scant illumination.

When they felt the tremors of another blast, they quickly moved to enter the opening. The tunnel floor shook gently under their feet, and they could feel the vibrations of earth and rocks falling somewhere behind them.

"Hurry!" panted Chris as he scrambled to join his father in the tunnel ahead. In his rush, he tripped and fell.

Suddenly the air around him grew thicker with the smell of rocky dust.

Chris shouted in horror. The flashlight held by Tom gave the tunnel behind him a nightmarish quality. Slowly, slowly the ceiling buckled and fell inward. Clouds of dust surrounded him as he lurched to his feet. The tremors grew more violent, and the ceiling above him cracked and heaved. He cried out hoarsely as the first rocks hit him.

Tom grabbed his son by the waist and pulled him through the narrow opening.

Rocks falling all around them, they fled the nightmare at their heels. Throwing themselves out of the passageway from which billows of dust spewed, they knelt and huddled together for protection.

They gradually became aware that the darkness had lessened, that all at once there was no ceiling to touch. A wave of fresh, unclouded air met their starving lungs, and they paused, gasping gratefully. They had entered the giant caverns under the cliffs.

NINE

THE O'REILLYS LOOKED UP AT THE great domed roof. Natural phosphorescence glowed gently from widely separated places in the ceiling and the walls. It gave an unearthly light to the echoing cavern in which they found themselves. Gradually, reference points in the cavern began to stand out as their eyes became used to the shadowy light.

The large hall was the length of a football field and as wide. Everywhere, great stalactites hung from the ceiling, while beneath them, in opposition, stalagmites grew up from the floor like huge fangs in the cavern's stony mouth.

The beauty was breathtaking as they looked around, and they were silent.

"It's like an underground palace," said Chris, finally giving voice to his fascination with the rainbow of shining lights on the glistening walls.

Gradually, they became aware of the silent traces of the Indians, which blended perfectly into their surroundings. Carved out of the stone-curtained columns of color that dominated the cavern, there stood an enormous chair. Below it, broad steps led up to the platform on which it rested.

Stone serpents twined about the top of the chair as if asleep.

"The kiva," said Tom. "Their ceremonial room. This would be where they had their important ceremonies, marriages and prayers to their god, the serpent."

Chris suddenly grinned. "Do you think the spirits of the Aztecs would put their curse on me if I sat on their throne?" He climbed up the long, flat steps to the magnificent chair and sat down, looking about him as a ruler might survey his subjects.

His father watched in amusement, recognizing in his son's humorous act the venting of tension in relief, a relief that he himself felt after leaving the suffocating tomb of caved-in rock.

With his dark tan and darker hair, Chris looked the part of an Aztec ruler. A scepter lay upon the broad arm of the throne, a length of gold metal hammered to a base of heavily polished stone and surmounted by a teardrop turquoise the measure of a fist in diameter. Minute, intricately carved serpents, frozen forever in their sinister coils, had been worked from the scepter's pure-gold handle.

Tom watched Chris pick up the scepter and wave it in the air.

"I am the all-powerful O'Reilly, ruler of the Aztecs," he intoned in a solemn voice and grinned again in the foolish exuberance of relief that had thrown caution to the winds.

A gentle hissing sound came from above his head as if steam were escaping from an opening somewhere.

Even in the dim half-light, Chris saw his father's face turn pale. "What is it?" he asked anxiously.

An ominous rattle seemed to fill the cavern, and Chris froze in unbelieving horror. In the dim light above his head, one of the five motionless snakes that had been twined about the top of the chair uncoiled and started to move.

"Chris, don't move a muscle!" Tom whispered urgently. "Diamondback!" he breathed, hypnotized by the lazy, flowing movement of the ugly, brown coils.

The snake paused above the boy, its loathsome head weaving from one side to the other as if to locate the thing that had awakened it. Seeing nothing to alarm it, the large snake oozed down the back of the chair toward the broad slab of stone where Chris's arm rested as if paralyzed.

The boy's back ached from the strain of sitting tensely upright. His first impulse had been to throw himself out of the chair and roll down the steps, but a look at Tom's white face had told him that the snake was too close.

Chris's lips trembled as he felt the snake touch his bare skin. The hairs of his arm tingled and stood upright as the smooth, moving skin of the rattler brushed them. Through his quivering, half-closed lashes, he caught the movement of a long, brown shape and tightly closed his eyes. He mustn't flinch. He held his breath.

As Tom watched, the five-foot snake flowed smoothly down the carved steps to the cavern floor. There it paused and at last headed for the opposite wall, where it disappeared into a low opening in the rock.

"Is it gone?" asked Chris weakly, opening his eyes.

Tom O'Reilly nodded, too overcome to speak. His eyes swept over the other four snakes coiled about the top of the throne. Yes, they were all carved from the stone. "We've got to use better judgment from now on," he admonished shakily, and his son nodded vehement agreement. They had been carried away by the elation of the moment. They mustn't let it happen again. Too much depended on their survival to risk their lives carelessly.

They began to work their way along the walls with the aid now of their flashlights.

They stepped through a doorway and entered a small room from which four separate tunnels branched off.

They entered the first tunnel to the left. After a short walk of twenty feet, it widened into a room.

There was a musty, rotting smell, the smell of grain that has been left too long. They shined their lights into a corner and found a pile of it, not much but enough to give off a pungent, musty odor.

In a corner of the room, stacked neatly in their places, lay an assortment of tools. Tools for tilling, tools for cutting, and tools for grinding grain. The farming implements stood unused against the wall, all of them carved from stone. They could have been laid down that afternoon after a hard morning's work; it was impossible to tell, for stone does not rust, does not easily show the passage of time, and would be as fresh one hundred years from now as it had been five hundred years before.

They retraced their steps to the small room that housed the entrances to the three remaining tunnels.

The second passage was so narrow that they could not walk abreast and proceeded cautiously in single file. Soon they became aware of large, dark openings along the wall. Hand-carved, roughly hewn doorways lined the tunnel on both sides. As they shined their lights inside one of them, they saw it was a small dwelling room.

They completed their inspection fully conscious that although a large and living community had once been settled there, the dwelling rooms now housed only forgotten items. The Indians had left the remnants of small fires and occasionally, in one room or another, small broken and abandoned cooking pots.

As they neared the end of the tunnel, Chris thought he heard a sound.

He whirled around and shined his light upon the wall. At that moment, he heard the click of rock on rock. A sound of closing. He carefully shined his light along the wall but found nothing to justify his feeling that he had been watched. And then the hairs rose on the back of his neck as his nostrils inhaled the unmistakable smell of animal skins and he sensed the intangible but recognizable presence of another human intelligence, which remained although the physical traces had disappeared.

"Did you hear that sound?" he asked breathlessly.

"Yes," affirmed Tom. His eyes searched the walls and tunnel but saw nothing. "Let's go," he said after a moment of utter silence as they strained their ears for alien sounds. "Deke must be getting close, if he hasn't blasted through already. We'll have to hurry. We have two more tunnels to explore."

After only six feet, the third tunnel widened into a room, spacious and circular. As their flashlights lit the walls, they became aware of the special human aspects of their surroundings.

Focused sharply by the bright light, vivid form and color leaped out at them from the walls. The naturally colored limestone had been divided into several parts, each part recessed into the wall and separate from the others. Slowly, Tom counted eight divisions, each a separately carved alcove ten feet long and, as the ceiling varied, up to twelve feet in height.

The beam of Tom's flashlight revealed scenes like those that archeologists had found within the tombs of pharaohs. Each of the alcoves held a mural that had been carved and colored by human hands into many rows of pictures. Excitement ran through Tom's body like electricity.

"A history of the Aztecs!" he exclaimed aloud.

In spite of their haste to escape the caverns, they hesitated. The murals seemed to hypnotize them. Almost against their will, they paused to inspect them. This, more than anything they had seen so far, made the lost tribe a group of living men and women with dreams and thoughts like other human beings. The two O'Reillys stood as if rooted to the spot.

Slowly the light followed the murals from alcove to alcove, and they gradually became aware that for eight different sections, there had been eight different artists.

Some images were delicate, some harsh, some heavy-handed, but all were precise and lifelike and as carefully drawn as the hand-inked volumes copied by monks during the Middle Ages.

Then it came to him. Eight alcoves, eight separate artists . . . eight different generations. He then began at the beginning with the first, most faded mural.

The rapt O'Reillys saw the journey from Mexico in color, faded with time but still hauntingly lifelike. The determined faces of men and women who carried their weaker children through the desert to seek out a new home and find protection from the horsemen who pursued them looked out at them with patient eyes.

They saw the Indians' discovery of the canyon with the serpentine river between its cliffs. The essence of the first alcove was the discovery of a new existence far from Mexico.

The next three generations showed a time of plenty. The farming skills they had brought with them from their native land were put to use in the barren canyon. The harvests, the feasts, the marriages, and the births of many children were celebrations of their success. Prosperity had been hard won, and now they could enjoy the fruits of their labors.

But when Tom's light stopped before the alcove that recorded the history of the fifth generation of canyon Aztecs, he paused, sick at heart, for he saw that the threat they had tried to leave behind in Mexico had returned to haunt them.

Beside him, his son was silent, caught by the spell of history.

Aided by the pictures on the wall, he saw it in his mind's eye. Ten soldiers, alone and probably deserters, swarthy, black-haired, bandoliered, and carrying rifles, had come upon a group of Aztec women as they tended their crops by the river. They took the women by surprise, but one escaped.

Warned by the young woman, the Aztec men came running. On the wall, frozen white puffs of smoke, which hung over the long, pointed sticks the soldiers carried, told a story of the desperately unequal battle; the piles of dead, both men and women, told of the terrible cost.

At last, the angry Aztecs overcame five of the intruders, whom they took captive. An Aztec court decreed an execution: death in a pit of vipers.

Tom shuddered, thinking of the horrible death which the murderers had so richly deserved, and stepped backward so that his flashlight might take in the next mural in its entirety.

His foot partially skidded at the edge of a crack in the stone. His flashlight picked up a large, rectangular rock, unmistakably a door, precisely cut and fitted to the cavern floor. He put his fingers into one of the longer cracks, and with Chris's help, the rock fell away, making them jump back to regain their balance.

The empty space below revealed a pit, ten feet deep and ten feet wide. At its bottom, the light bounced off five gleaming lengths of skeleton, and he understood with a shudder that this had been the execution pit.

The bones were mingled carelessly with the long spinal remains of many vipers. A sudden movement in response to light caught his eye. The beam cast ugly shadows behind the squat, triangular, living heads of poisonous serpents as they lay coiled on the bare bones of their victims.

Chris nodded to himself. The serpent had been an especially fitting symbol for the tribe. Like their fanged protector, the Indians had been harmless, even shy, when left alone. But they had struck out with deadly force when molested by intruders.

The next three murals, representing the one hundred years following the execution, revealed that the population of the tribe had been almost wiped out. The times of plenty had become times of hardship. The artists' skillful hands grew angry and harsh. Those surviving now had sterner faces. Few children were born.

The last mural was left unfinished. It told of Andrew and his father, of Deke, and of a younger Tom O'Reilly.

Tom turned to his son, a strange, excited look in his eyes. The words came slowly. "Back at the cabin when you heard Andrew talk about the Aztec and his cat, you must have thought the old man had been seeing things. An old man's delusions, you must have thought, as simple and sad as that. And I can't blame you. But twenty-five years ago, I was a young man of seventeen, with perfect eyesight and no tendency to fantasize."

Chris stood motionless, his eyes widening as he saw what Tom was driving at. "You saw them too?" he asked incredulously.

"When I opened my eyes after the fall, I knew that I was badly hurt. I lay on the riverbank, soaking wet, with my right arm feeling as if it were being pinched in half by white-hot scissors and my head much too broken and heavy to lift. My leg was bent at a painful angle and felt numb. My vision slowly cleared, and when it did, what I saw made me start to leap to my feet. At least, that's what my body tried to do. But the searing, agonizing pain that shot up my leg to my back sent me back into oblivion for many minutes.

"When I awoke again, it was a pitch-dark, moonless night, and I was lying only ten feet from Andrew's door as helpless as before. When I realized where I was and how impossible it would have been for me to get there on my own, the vision I'd seen at the foot of the cliff came back to me with blinding force: a tall, slender Indian, erect with dignity, his black, shining hair worn long. A turquoise necklace with a hundred pear-shaped stones hung from his slender neck almost to his hips. He wore a short loincloth of brown rabbit fur and moccasins. He carried no weapons. In the instant his eyes met mine, I saw no animosity in his gaze. It was a look of concern mixed with aloofness and the fleeting emotions of shyness and hope. Later, safe and warm in Andrew's cabin, I put the vision down to that blow on the head I had sustained on the cliff."

Tom smiled wryly. "I decided that in a semiconscious state I had swum to shore and later crawled the long way to the cabin by myself. Anything else was preposterous. I dismissed as fancy the fact that this stranger had rescued me from the river and carried me home. I never mentioned it to Andrew. Tonight, when I heard him tell us of his canyon ghosts, I knew that his image of the Indian, minus the aging brought by twenty-five years, was identical with my own."

"Do you think . . . ?" began Chris in a voice choked with excitement.

91

"I know." Tom spoke decisively. "There is a Survivor in the canyon, a lone Aztec, perhaps the last of a great, proud tribe."

"It's too bad he never came out to meet Andrew. They would have understood each other," said Chris, still feeling shivery at the thought of a flesh-and-blood inhabitant of these ghostly cold and barren caverns.

"I think he's wanted to for years," Tom said softly, "but the sacred duty passed on to him by his tribe made it very hard to break away from tradition. He wanted very much to make a link to the outside world. That's why he let me see him twenty-five years ago and why he showed himself to Andrew so many times, too shy to come very close, always staying in the shadows. He planted that golden serpent at Andrew's fishing hole himself as an act of friendship. But when he saw that Andrew had spotted his reflection in the water, he knew that he was still afraid and disappeared again as the storm broke."

"So he stayed inside these walls," said Chris, thinking sadly of all the wasted years.

Tom nodded. "And Andrew and I stuck our heads in the sand like ostriches. I, because I wouldn't believe my own eyes; Andrew, because he knew he wanted to see him more than anything else in the world and couldn't stand the possibility of finding out that he'd created him out of his imagination."

"Dad," Chris spoke in a hushed tone, "if the Survivor saved your life before, does it mean he's friendly to us now?"

Tom shook his head. "I don't know, Son. You see, now we're trespassers, not innocent people who need help. He may feel that he must defend his home."

Chris looked toward the Spaniards in the pit and shuddered. He raised his eyes to the mural again and nodded, understanding that the man who had saved his father's life twenty-five years before was the final historian of the Aztec tribe.

He looked uneasily around him at the silent walls, half expecting to see the sudden apparition of the Aztec regarding him in thoughtful silence, but they were still alone in the room, the only witnesses to the history of a once-great civilization. He turned back to finish reading the mural.

A man who wore a necklace of many turquoise stones stood all alone in a vast, empty space. The sadness of the lines that formed the figure hit Chris forcibly. A sad, imprisoned face following the destiny decreed for it by the tribe's tradition, a tradition that would never let go.

He studied the last mural and wondered how the Aztec could bear to be the final keeper of the history and the gold. He understood that the creators of the murals had tried to keep the essence of their tribe alive, to soften the harsh existence they had chosen in living underground. But nothing can soften an act of self-destruction. The caverns had become a tomb, and the epitaph could only be inside the grave.

Chris stirred uneasily, feeling again that he was being watched, and slowly passed the beam of light over the murals that surrounded him. He saw a portrait, carved and chiseled with the greatest care, of what must have been the founder of the canyon Indians. What he saw in the old Aztec's face made him turn pale.

"Look!" he whispered hoarsely, the flashlight shaking in his hand. He forced himself to steady it.

The face was empty, not only of any expression of the stoic pride that characterized most great Indian leaders but of that which makes expression possible. He knew with a dread certainty that only moments before those empty sockets had been filled with living flesh, that the Survivor himself had been watching him warily from behind the carved protection of another face.

Tom stepped to the wall opposite the tunnel by which they had entered. There was another passage there. "This way," he said and stepped cautiously inside.

The sense of being watched vanished. The tunnel sloped gradually through the tons of heavy rock. It was high and wide like the others. Held firmly in place by small, carved shelves, half-burned torches stood upright against the wall, head high, at regular intervals.

There were hand-carved niches in the walls such as those found in churches holding icons. These held the icon peculiar to the Indian tribe, the serpent, and each coiled statue was made of shining gold. Ahead of his son, Tom O'Reilly paused to look but didn't touch them before he hurried on.

At a curving bend of the tunnel, he faced another niche. This one held the most spectacular treasure of all, and he stopped in fascination. It was filled with piles of turquoise jewelry and golden jars and statues, like the window of a jeweler's store.

Chris stood close beside his father and, with an exclamation of real pleasure, tried to lift a small golden vase. It was very heavy. With some surprise, he found that it could be moved only to one side, the length of the display case, a distance of nearly four feet. Its base was firmly embedded in the rock and could not be removed. He stood and admired it wordlessly.

"Come on, Son; time's running out," said Tom, gently pushing him forward.

The action of shifting the vase had begun a chain of events planned and created long before by a tribal architect bent on protecting the treasure of his tribe from all outsiders. Several feet away in the floor of the passageway they would take on their way out, a slab of rock slid aside. A portion of the solid floor became the blackness of a shaft. The echoing sound of Tom's voice covered the grating sound of stone on stone.

Chris's eyes were still on the small, exquisite treasure. Followed by his father, he stepped toward the hole, well hidden from detection in the shadow of the curve.

Suddenly, he felt the fierceness of bony fingers clutch his arm above the elbow, holding him in place with sinewy strength, and his whole body jumped with the electricity of fear. Behind him, he heard his father's gasp of shock. He whirled around to see who had him.

A choking cry cut off in his throat as he looked into the eyes of the Survivor.

Silently, the Aztec pointed ahead to the hole in the floor inches away from the boy's extended foot and then, skirting the hole, stepped forward to the end of the passageway to another display case. He shifted a golden vase there in the same way Chris had moved the first, and the slab of rock slowly reappeared.

Chris and Tom O'Reilly stood as still as statues. The Survivor stood silently watching them from the end of the passageway.

No words were spoken, but no words were necessary. If he could have spoken the O'Reillys' language, the Survivor would have said, "I know that you are honest men. You didn't take the gold; you only looked at it. My ancestors made me the keeper of the treasure; but in guarding it, I am also the keeper of justice, and these traps were meant only to protect us against evil men, not to harm men such as you. . . ."

None of this was said aloud, but sometimes there may pass through human eyes a current of understanding that bonds two human minds.

In his wrinkled brown face, they sensed that he had made an irrevocable decision, a decision that would consciously change the course of the Aztec legend . . . voluntary contact with outsiders.

Suddenly, Chris understood the reason for this choice. He knew the Aztec now understood that in the outer world there were men of other tribes who would respect his property, and the boy felt a sense of pride that he and his father had given him that example. They felt a moment of history and the close of an era, the finish to the tribe's dark ages.

The O'Reillys watched the rock as it finished sliding back into place. Before their eyes, the floor once again became a safe passageway. When they looked up, they found they were alone.

"Where did he go, Dad?" asked Chris. "He saved me from a bad fall, and then he disappeared again. I thought he'd stay now. I thought he'd help us out of here."

The muffled sound of an explosion shook the rock.

"We're not the only trespassers right now," said Tom

grimly. "He's gone to watch Deke and his friends. He's warned us that there are traps ahead. Now it's up to us to protect ourselves. We'll be on guard from now on. Don't worry, Son," he said gently, a look of quiet excitement in his eyes. "The Survivor will come back. I saw it too, that look in his eyes. We'll see him again. When all of this is over."

"Traps ahead?" asked Chris, still dazed from the encounter. "Of course. That hole in the floor . . . I caused it by pulling the vase to one side. It must be attached to that slab by ropes. And when the Survivor wanted to close it, he just went to the other end of the hallway and pulled it shut by moving the other vase in the opposite direction. It was attached to the slab too with another set of ropes."

Tom nodded. His face grew serious. "We'll have to keep our eyes open. It's up to us now. Our friend, the Aztec, will be too busy with Deke and his gang to help us again."

The tunnel ceiling sloped lower as they followed the burnt-out torches. After ten yards, it had become so low that they had to bend double to move along. It was difficult to walk this way without bumping their heads, and the going was slow. The tunnel was twice as long as any of the others, and again they began to have difficulty in catching their breath.

The ceiling abruptly rose to a considerable height.

Ahead of his father, Chris gasped with surprise. Shakily, he lined up his flashlight on the sight that had unnerved him.

Carved from the cavern stone at the end of the tunnel was a most unusual doorway. The opening was more than unusual; it was bizarre and chilling and directly in keeping with the theme that had assaulted their senses after they had been forced to enter the Aztec's domain.

It was a giant serpent's head with grotesquely exaggerated fangs above and below. Whoever entered the room beyond must pass between its gaping jaws. Slanted snake's eyes fired by ruby-red gems glared down at them, daring them to enter.

Silently and very cautiously, they stepped between the giant jaws. Beyond the serpent gate lay a silent cavern as large and as beautiful as the throne room. But the objects that held their attention most weren't made of stone.

On long ledges which had been deeply carved into the walls lay the bony remains of the missing Aztec tribe. The remains were dressed in what must have been their finest clothing, and here and there, bits of moldy feathers clustered around the skeletal heads. At the foot of each skeleton lay a pile of personal belongings.

The O'Reillys walked through the tomb feeling as if they were in slow motion. Time stood still for them in the silent cavern; it was eerie to be alone underground, surrounded by the hollow stares of skeletons, unfriendly stares it seemed to them. "Trespassers!" the open, bony mouths seemed to hiss in a silence like that of a loaded gun.

Chris studied the scene. "I wonder why they died. Do you think a disease might have killed them all at once?" he whispered.

"Maybe." Tom answered slowly in the same quiet tone. "But maybe not. What if the Indians got sick at heart, living underground all the time. They were used to living outside under the sun, which they used to worship as a god because it gave them health and growth and life. They could have lost the will to live down here."

"The will to live." Tom's own thought echoed in his mind as his eye caught the figure of an Aztec skeleton against the wall, sitting proudly upright as if it had refused to acknowledge the claims of death.

There was something forbidding in its pose, as if its owner had sat down centuries before in order to wait for the trespassers he knew would come. The skeleton was composed in an attitude of patient waiting and certainty, knowing that the boldness of the trespassers would be frustrated. The proud head sat regally on straight shoulders, and the whole body leaned against a wall of rock.

Tom focused his flashlight on the wall behind the skeleton. "There's something special about this rock; there must be. This is the only upright skeleton in the room. It's almost forbidding us to go any farther."

"As if we could go farther," said Chris. "We've reached the end of this trail. It looks like a dead end."

"Unless . . . ." said his father as his flashlight followed a thin crack in the wall behind the skeleton, a crack that outlined a doorway in the rock.

"A door!" exclaimed Chris, his voice lifting with sudden hope. "I wonder how it opens."

They examined it from a distance, held in place by the hypnotic, hollow stare of the old Aztec.

"There are no visible handles, grooves, or pulleys," said Tom thoughtfully. "But it must operate on some system of weights and balances."

Ignoring the skeleton's fierce gaze, they approached the door. For ten minutes, while the beams of their flashlights grew noticeably dimmer, they pushed and felt and slid their anxious hands along the crack in vain.

"But this *is* a door!" muttered Chris. He leaned on the rectangular rock and pushed again with all his might. "It won't budge. It has to open somehow."

"The means of opening it are hidden," said Tom thoughtfully. "The Aztecs knew how to open it, but they intended that no one but themselves should know. Something very important to them is on the other side of that door; otherwise they wouldn't have placed their guardian in front of it." He caught his breath at a sudden thought. "If you were an Aztec," he said excitedly to his son, "how would you conceal something important from outsiders, maybe a treasure the world was hounding you for? According to your beliefs and superstitions, what would prevent your enemies from opening this door?"

Chris paused, puzzled, and then his face brightened. "I think you have something. The Indians believed strongly in the power of their spirits after death. That's why each warrior was laid to rest in his finest clothing with his weapons at his feet for hunting in the afterlife and his pottery beside him for cooking. If they believed their spirits were powerful enough to overcome trespassers after their gold . . . ." His gaze wandered to where the old Aztec sat, his bony body rigid and forbidding, his wispy white hair cradling his skull against the door's rocky base, a kind of chair. "Of course!" he breathed. "The only place it could be."

He bent to the skeleton and placed his two hands on either bony shoulder. The bone was smooth and cold and surprisingly light as he gently pushed the body to one side until it crumpled unresistingly upon the cold rock floor with the hollow clicking sound of rattling bones. He lifted the long, thin legs, still encased in rotting animal skins, until the skeleton was clear of the space it had occupied. There, beneath the body, was the answer.

In a cavity hollowed out in the stone, there lay a golden statue about one foot long.

Chris lifted it out. It was very heavy. He examined it silently for a moment. Then he turned it upside down. Its base was six inches square, and in it there was a deep hole.

He looked around him at the rows of dead Indians. "This statue is a key," he told his father. "It fits over something. Somehow, it's meant to open that door. I know it."

"Looks that way to me too," said Tom. "Now we have to find the lock." He stepped back to study the door and the surrounding walls. Suddenly, he smiled. On either side of the door was an alcove like the ones in the passageway. Each alcove had an arrangement of golden plates and weapons and jewelry, but only one of them had a golden statue. It was exactly like the one Chris held in his hands.

Tom walked to the other alcove, the one without the statue, and looked down at the place where it should have been. There it was, a hole the width of the statue's base and three feet long. Within the hole, he saw a peg with a rope around it,

Tom looked at Chris with an excited grin. "The statue fits over the peg. Remember how the trapdoor worked in the passageway?"

Chris nodded. There was a sparkle in his eyes as he set the statue over the peg in the hole.

With an effort that took all of their combined

strength, they pulled the statue along its track. Before their watchful eyes, the door of rock slid aside with a low, grating sound.

A six-foot tunnel stretched before them, widening into a small cavern. They shined their lights into the tunnel ahead and stepped past the skeleton of the Aztec chieftain into the tunnel.

Suddenly, they heard the movement of rock behind them.

"Watch out, it's closing!" shouted Tom, whirling around.

The two of them turned and squeezed through the slowly narrowing entranceway just in time. As they watched in consternation, the block of stone settled again into place. The skeleton beside it seemed to grin up at them from its position on the floor.

Chris shivered as he stared back into the still, white skull. Then he looked at the statue in the alcove. Its position had slipped back and allowed the door to close. "It's no trap, Dad," he said. "We just didn't open the door to the proper position."

"This time we'll make sure it's open to stay," Tom said firmly. With Chris's help, he pulled the statue to the end of its track. Together, they watched it. It didn't move.

"That's got it, now," said Chris, grinning with relief. "For a moment there, I started to believe in ghosts again."

Tom chuckled in appreciation. "All right, let's go and find that treasure!"

Cautiously and abnormally aware that the planning and intelligence of long-dead men still loomed about them as a threat, they entered.

Their eyes widened, although they had known what they would find.

The Aztec treasure. It could have been nothing else.

There were mountains of golden cups and plates. Beautiful jewels, dim with age, peeped out from golden cases. Piles of turquoise flashed blue in the light. Earthenware pottery, painted in bright colors, held necklaces and rings in shining profusion, and little statues made of gold stood upright along the wall. Near the entrance, ceremonial armor and ornate weaponry added to the splendor.

"So the legend really is true!" Chris stood entranced. He bent down to slip a golden serpent ring on his finger. It was a perfect fit. He held it out into the light, admiring its craftsmanship.

He paused, the expression of delight slowly fading from his face. A quiet look of apprehension replaced it. "Do you think there's anything to that ancient curse on the gold?" he asked his father uneasily, suddenly feeling the deathlike silence of the cavern close in around them. "You've got to admit that it's been pretty well protected until now."

"You know better than to believe in a curse," said Tom. "Its only intended function is to scare people into believing that something terrible will happen to them if they dare to go against it. Get back!" he cried suddenly as he trained his light on the mound of gold in front of his son's outstretched hand.

Chris had been in the act of removing the golden serpent ring. Now he leaped back in response to the command.

For the second time that night, they heard a warning rattle. It came ominously from the piles of shining treasure. From behind a large vase, a diamondback's ugly, brown head appeared. Then another serpent slithered out from beneath a smiling golden mask. Both reptiles were sleek and fat and looked as if they had been purposely fed and cared for as fitting guardians for the treasure. Their evil heads cast weaving shadows on the cavern wall behind them.

Chris caught his breath in the sudden, horrifying thought that here, in response to a summons from the long-dead Aztec tribe, appeared the vengeant devils of an Aztec god. A strike from their wickedly curving fangs would ensure a painful end.

The O'Reillys didn't wait for a second look. With one accord, they whipped around to run back through the six-foot tunnel into the burial chamber and ran into a solid wall of rock.

Dazed, they heard the sound of rattling grow as if more snakes had joined the deadly chorus. They turned this way and that, the beams of their flashlights making wild arcs on the walls of the small chamber. The door was firmly back in place. In their excitement at finding the treasure, they had not heard it close. Shocked at the discovery, they stood together at the end of the short tunnel, fumbling helplessly along the walls for another means of exit but finding none.

The rattling stopped.

Slowly, their breathing returned to almost normal, and they began to think. Tom backed away from the door to study it. By the side of the tunnel wall, he saw two protruding stone serpents' heads. A quick flash of the light into the treasure room illuminated the horrifying sight of serpents moving soundlessly in their direction, a silence infinitely more terrifying than the nerve-wracking, rattling sound of warning.

Together, their shaking hands caught hold of the ugly stone fangs and pushed and pulled with frantic strength. Something in the wall gave way. The serpent head Chris was pushing slid suddenly to one side. A loud click was answered by a low, muffled rumbling beneath their feet. Too late they realized what was coming.

The key stone which was the serpent's head had shifted. Now the stone beneath their feet, no longer tightly held in place, began to move.

With no further warning, the floor beneath them dropped away, clattering and spinning down the hole and giving them no time to place their feet on firmer rock. Their flashlights flew into the air and landed somewhere in the snake-infested room behind them.

Feet first, they dropped into a tunnel, smoothed and curved and aimed relentlessly downward. In darkness black as pitch, sound became their only guide. Their momentum increased. They had no time to think beyond their terror, but at the edge of their consciousness, growing louder, came a noise they could not recognize, which grew and grew. Suddenly, feet first, they shot through the blackness into a realm of dim, gray light, a light so faint that they could barely make out shapes around them.

Before their fall came abruptly to an end, they understood that they had fallen into a tremendous cavern, like a cathedral, barely illuminated by phosphorescence in the walls above and filled with a rumbling sound like the wind of a great hurricane. And as they fell into a breath-stopping coldness, they knew it was caused by the dark and rushing force of a river roaring underground.

They hit the rushing river and disappeared within the blankets of white foam that rose above its sleek, shining surface like instantly vanishing puffs of smoke.

TEN

THE BLACK, ROARING RIVER LOOKED evil as it washed the struggling human forms away. It looked like a writhing, shining serpent devouring its prey and did not remotely resemble that other peaceful, light-blue river which flowed calmly between the towering cliffs of Cougar Canyon on the other side of the wall.

Two white faces rushed toward a wall laced with foam as the water hit it and charged through the cavernous channel beneath it.

Tom caught the edge of the channel and gasped for breath. "Hang on!" he shouted to his son and watched him cling to the wall, fighting for breath. He knew that the violent subterranean tunnel must join the peaceful Pecos River on the other side, but he did not know how far they would be pushed and pulled and tugged through the suffocating channel, unable to draw a breath, or whether they would be knocked unconscious against a protruding rock. They could not take the chance.

It was like trying to move through molasses, thought Chris as he hooked his fingers into small cracks in the rock face above him and pulled his shivering body through the current which held him against the wall. He moved with infinite slowness toward a long, flat rock which lay fifteen feet away at the river's edge.

The river's echoing roar beat into his ears, and he paused, coughing and choking with the unending spray which repeatedly filled his mouth with water. Over all the sounds, his father's strong, calm voice gave him the determination not to give in to the insistent tug of the current and flow with it under the wall.

At last, he pulled himself out onto the rock. He turned and held out an arm to his father.

Exhausted from the effort, they lay quietly amid the small, cold pools of water that dripped from their soaked clothing.

Suddenly, they heard a loud, sharp crack like a rifle shot and stood up, their exhausted muscles responding reluctantly and much too slowly. Clouds of dust fanned out toward them from the wall that separated them from the canyon outside.

As they stood rooted to the spot, expecting momentarily to be covered by an avalanche of rocks, the dust diminished, and in its place a large, pale rectangle of early-morning light appeared as if by magic.

They stared unbelievingly at this miraculous escape route, created instantly as if it had been the direct result of a wish. Still unbelievingly, they watched three brawny figures step through the light into the cavern.

With sinking hearts, they knew they'd lost the race as they recognized Deke, Sully, and Dutch. Deke stiffened as he saw them. An unpleasant grimace made his face a snarl, and it was obvious that he had considered them an obstacle already disposed of.

Tom and Chris stood quietly, each calculating the chances of escape from this new danger.

Strapped to Deke's waist was a holster and gun, and they knew that the stakes were so great that he wouldn't hesitate to use the weapon against them. They remained still and waited for Mahler to make the first move.

Sully, too, wore a gun. Dutch was the only one among the three who had no weapon. The wielding of a gun required a mind, and it was obvious to anyone with eyes that Dutch was just a hulking mound of human flesh to be used as a robot by his masters. The giant carried a pile of heavy knapsacks.

Deke began to laugh unpleasantly as he walked toward the O'Reillys. "Houdini could take lessons from you two," he declared in a rumbling voice which carried easily over the noise of the river. "That was the greatest disappearing act I ever saw. You sure convinced Andrew. We left him sitting outside, tied up. He hasn't said a word since you disappeared." He eyed them speculatively.

Tom's jaw tightened, but still he said nothing. It was cold in the cavern. He was soaking wet from falling into the river and had begun to shiver. The cold penetrated his mind, and his thoughts grew clearer, like stars on a cold, clear night.

Chris remained quiet, taking his cue from his father. He too was shaking with the cold. The icy water hadn't left a shred of dry clothing on his body, and he hugged himself, rubbing his arms with shaking hands.

With an exclamation, Deke reached out and caught Chris's right hand, jerking it forward so roughly that the boy stumbled off balance.

The Aztec serpent ring, which Chris in his fear of

the advancing rattlers in the treasure room had not had time to remove, glimmered and shone under the insistent glare of the flashlight and was reflected in Mahler's greedy eyes.

"Where did you get this?" Deke demanded roughly.

Without answering, Chris tried to withdraw his hand, which Deke in his enthusiasm was crushing rather cruelly.

Tom intervened. "Let him go," he said quietly but firmly.

Deke stepped back, drew his gun, and noted with a sadistic grin the fear in Tom O'Reilly's eyes.

But he had misread Tom's expression. What he thought was fear was sudden thoughtfulness, a vision of the traps lining the corridors in the maze of passageways above. The Aztecs' traps, prepared for criminals who chose to steal their gold. Instantly, Tom had realized that their best chance lay in herding Deke toward his just rewards.

Tom looked across at Chris, hoping he would follow his cue without questions or surprised looks which might make Deke suspicious. This had to be handled delicately, for Mahler was an intelligent man, not a creature like Dutch who could be twisted into any shape a smart man wished.

"Tell him. Tell him where the treasure is," he urged in a shaky, nervous voice. The shivering which had come from being wet only heightened his act. His eyes bored into Chris's to tell him silently that he had a reason unconnected with the waiting muzzle of the gun.

Deke looked at him with surprise mingled with contempt but seemed to find nothing unusual about a man who cringed before a gun.

Chris hesitated, then pointed to the ceiling. "That hole leads to the treasure room. I don't know any other way to get up there."

"He's telling the truth," said Tom quickly as the gun moved forward menacingly. "But there must be another way up from here. If you look around, you might find it."

Deke looked from one earnest face to another. Then he turned to Sully. "Get busy. Look for a tunnel somewhere. One that leads up." He seized Chris's finger again and tugged at the ring, nearly dislocating the wrist as he twisted the ring off.

Chris didn't make a sound, but his blazing eyes spoke for him as he stared down at the floor. They said things he didn't want Deke Mahler to see just yet. For a while, he would remain passive because his father seemed to have a plan. But the urge for justice seethed inside him, and looking over at his father, he caught the same tense and steely look in those green eyes.

The group stood without speaking as Sully paced the cavern. "I think I've found it, Boss," he shouted almost inaudibly above the roar after a search of minutes. He pointed toward the black shadow of what looked like the open mouth of a tunnel leading upward through the rock.

"All right, Dutch," ordered Deke, "pass out the knapsacks. We're going to fill them up with gold! You too, O'Reillys!"

Moments later, they all entered the tunnel, passing

111

beneath another carved replica of the serpent-god.

Tom unobtrusively took a tiny object from his inner jacket pocket and held it in his palm. It had been well protected by a piece of oiled cloth from the river's force. He pressed a switch.

Beside Deke's flare, Tom's tiny flashlight paled to insignificance. Still, he kept it on as insurance. Should something happen to Deke, he didn't want Chris and himself left without a source of light in those dark passageways. And he was determined that something was indeed going to happen to Deke Mahler and his companions.

Chris suddenly thought he knew what his father had in mind. He guessed they had entered the fourth and last tunnel, leading back to the room outside the kiva where all the tunnels began. They had never had a chance to explore this tunnel. Once they reached the tunnel room, he believed that his father planned to guide Deke and his men through the third tunnel to the mural room and to the waiting traps ahead.

He shivered with excitement and then caught his breath. What if this tunnel were booby-trapped too?

"Dad, be careful!" Chris whispered.

Ahead of him, Tom nodded.

"Be quiet, you two!" growled Deke.

They climbed carefully upward, the tunnel sloping rather sharply at times, but they saw nothing suspicious.

Entering the tunnel room, Chris breathed a sigh of relief. Now they were on familiar ground.

Deke eyed the three other tunnel openings. "Which way?" Sully and Dutch shuffled nervously by his side.

Chris smiled to himself. If they were nervous now,

just wait until they saw the snakes . . . if they got that far.

"The third tunnel will take us to the treasure," answered Tom solemnly.

After only a few steps, the tunnel curved and widened into the mural room. Deke entered behind the O'Reillys. His eyes widened when he saw the pictures. "What's this?" he asked.

"It's the complete history of a lost culture," said Chris sternly. "It tells how the Aztecs of this tribe died out because of men like you," he added, his sense of justice forcing the words harshly from his mouth.

Deke sneered. "Never mind that. Where's the gold?"

"This way." Tom gestured to the tunnel opening on the far side of the room. "After you."

"Oh no. You first. If you're thinking of pulling anything, forget it. We're watching your every move. Get going."

Tom shrugged and ducked under the low doorway. He slowly increased his pace, Chris doing the same, until the distance between the two groups had widened to ten feet. They passed the first Aztec display case. Chris looked back. Deke and Sully had stopped to rob the alcove of its treasure. Nothing happened. No door opened beneath them to swallow them up. He hid his disappointment. The Aztecs had not used all the gold as bait.

"Keep on going, but be careful," whispered Tom as Chris passed him on the way to the second alcove with Dutch marching robotlike behind him.

At the breathtaking display at the entrance to the curve, Tom quickly moved the golden statue in its track. The stone slid silently away in the shadow of the tunnel floor ahead.

Chris rounded the curve, followed closely by a determined Dutch, and stepped aside, hugging the wall. The giant followed, panting, and saw the hole too late. Like an ox overcome by the momentum of its own weight on the edge of a cliff, he stumbled in and disappeared from sight with a howl of fear.

All of it had taken only seconds. As Chris stepped back around the curve, he ran into Deke.

Deke peered around the corner, but the light illuminated an empty passageway. Chris's body hid the trap momentarily from sight. "Where's Dutch?" His eyes narrowed suspiciously as he watched the boy lean innocently against the wall.

"Maybe he was gotten by the Aztec spirits," said Chris seriously. "There really are ghosts here, you know."

"Don't be stupid," muttered Deke. "We made up that story for my uncle. Dutch!" he bellowed. The echo rebounded from the walls of the empty tunnel and finally receded without an answer, leaving a hum on the air.

"He can't be far ahead," suggested Tom, a look of satisfaction in his eyes. "We'll catch up with him."

"Yeah," muttered Sully. "Let's go. This place is giving me the creeps."

From behind Chris came a muffled yell. Deke stiffened. "What was that?"

Chris reluctantly stepped away from the hole.

The sound came again.

"Dutch?" The look of surprise on Deke's face was almost comical.

"Boss!" An anguished whine came faintly from below. "My foot's broke!"

"We left some rope outside in the canyon, Boss," said Sully, turning to go.

"Wait a minute." Deke's voice was hard. "The big ox can stay where he is. We have better things to do than waste our time hauling him up at the end of a rope."

Sully grinned slowly. "Yeah. And divvying up that treasure two ways instead of three makes a lot more sense to me."

"All right." Deke gestured with the gun. "You O'Reillys back out in front. If there are any more traps, you're going to be the guinea pigs this time."

They walked slowly down the passageway, avoiding the hole. The howls of the trapped man grew faint; then they could hear nothing but the echoes of their own footsteps.

It wasn't far now to the gold. Rounding the last curve, Chris searched his mind for memories of the tunnel. But there before him loomed the awesome jaws of the serpent guardian to the burial chamber. Grimly, he realized that once they had the gold, Deke's gang wouldn't need their captives anymore except perhaps to carry their booty back out into the canyon.

His eyes widened. There before him lay another trap. How had they missed it the first time they walked this way? He looked carefully around him. A shiver traveled up his spine and lodged unmoving at the base of his neck as he realized it had not been there before.

Spread across the floor a few yards away lay a dark brown net, almost invisible in the half-light. A woven leather rope was attached to each corner of the net. Chris's eyes followed the ropes upward.

Far above, he saw a wooden platform. The ropes led through a hole in the center of it and wound around two boulders balanced on opposite sides of the platform. The huge stones looked as if they would fall at the slightest touch. What was preventing them from falling right on top of everybody?"

Then he saw how the trap was going to work. A thick rope joined the boulders across the platform, and if this rope were cut, the weights would fall and jerk the net up to the ceiling.

He caught his breath. Standing like a statue between the boulders was a human figure. The Survivor. The Indian's arm was raised, and in his hand, Chris saw a knife. Even in the shadows above, its sharp edge glinted in reflection of the flashlights below.

Chris lowered his eyes. The tunnel's shadows were more than adequate to shade the sight from the eyes of approaching intruders. That and the first awesome meeting with the serpent-god.

Chris slowed his steps. When the knife above fell to cut the rope that held the boulders in place, he intended to be out of the way.

Tom had seen the trap too. He edged toward the side of the path, letting Deke and Sully have full view of the doorway as they approached it.

It was a perfect setup and Sully fell for it.

"Boss, look at those rubies!" he yelled, beside himself with excitement as he lunged forward to relieve the serpent's eyes of their angry, glittering gems.

His foot stepped squarely into the center of the net.

Chris looked up. He saw the knife descend and cut the rope in two. The boulders tipped over the edge of the platform. The ropes followed the weights, swiftly drawing up the corners of the net.

Sully was suddenly surrounded by a snare of dark brown netting. The trap ascended, pulled upward by the great weight of the falling rocks to which it was attached. Their weight jerked Sully upward as if he were a feather in the wind.

Deke leaped back in shocked amazement. His mouth hung open in disbelief. He watched as Sully was lifted quickly to the high, dark ceiling above, a screaming cocoon of leather netting. The boulders knocked loudly against the sides of the passageway as they fell and came to rest on the floor beside them. With a bump, Sully hit against the bottom of the platform. His furious struggles were of no use. He hung there like a fish in a net.

"It's a booby-trap!" whispered Deke unbelievingly.

"Boss!" shrieked Sully far above. "Help!"

Chris looked above Sully to where the Survivor had been. He saw a shadow move.

Deke saw it too. "There's somebody up there!" he yelled and fired his gun at the platform.

The bullets whistled by Sully and hit the wood of the platform. Sully screamed.

Deke paused, a look of fear on his face.

The moving shadow had vanished. The only movement and sound in the cavern now was Sully swinging in his net and moaning with fear.

"Do you believe in ghosts now, Deke?" asked Tom in a whisper.

Deke turned to the O'Reillys. His body was trembling with fear, but his face was a mask of greedy determination. "How far is it to the gold?" he demanded in a low, ugly voice.

"Just through this next room," answered Tom quietly.

Passing through the awesome doorway with Sully's desperate cries for help still ringing in their ears, Chris and Tom went immediately to the alcove and pulled the golden statue along its track. They looked at each other with serious eyes, each one thinking the same thought: this was their last chance to get rid of Deke. The trapdoor, which had sent them headlong into the river, would still be open. Maybe they could manage to push him over the edge. And if that failed, the snakes. Maybe Deke would be unprepared for the snakes.

The door slid open. Chris held his breath. But Deke's flashlight picked up the open hole at once. He chuckled nastily. "That's one trap I won't fall into," he said, pushing Chris ahead of him so suddenly that the boy lost his balance.

Tom caught his son before his fall could send him down the hole. Behind them, they heard the big man breathe more quickly with excitement as he saw the treasure.

"It's here! The lost gold! There must be millions!" All business now, Deke gestured with his gun to the O'Reillys to begin picking up all that they could carry. Even at the appearance of the first rattlesnake, Deke showed no hesitation. His unblinking, wary eyes searched out all obstacles to the wealth before him, and with four bullets from his gun, he killed them all and kicked their writhing bodies aside.

Remembering the way they'd left the cave the first

time, Chris stood a heavy shield in the path of the door. Moments later, it stopped the moving rock on its way across and lodged it firmly open.

It took only twenty minutes for the three of them to load themselves with all the treasure they could carry. Deke's pockets bulged with Aztec jewelry, his fingers glittered with rings, and swinging turquoise necklaces dangled heavily around his shoulders. In the large knapsacks they had brought especially for the purpose, each of them packed golden statues and utensils. The load was almost more than they could carry.

Cold, wet, and tired, Tom O'Reilly limped the way back through the tunnel toward the river cavern. His still-soaking clothes clung to his shivering body and pulled coldly across his chest with every step.

Chris followed, his eyes searching the paths ahead for further traps. Hopelessly, he knew that even if they encountered one, Deke Mahler was no fool and was even more wary and determined now that he had the gold. He knew the slightest unusual movement from either of them would be greeted by a shout of anger at the least and, at the most, a bullet in the back.

Chris saw that underneath his ruthless determination, Deke Mahler was afraid of the supernatural powers he believed had disposed of his two friends and that the white-knuckled finger on the trigger of his gun was ready to react to any sudden threat. Deke's watchful eyes darted suspiciously from one corner of the tunnel to another as he pushed Chris, who was nearest, roughly along.

"Hurry up!" Deke barked.

Without further excitement, they once again entered the river room. Once again, their ears were flooded with the roaring of a river gone wild as the echoing sound burst upon them.

All at once, a detonation cracked the air, sending waves of singing sound through the cavern like the vibrations of a giant tuning fork.

The air was split by a thunderous crack as the ceiling broke inward. The O'Reillys ran back into a corner of the cavern as far from the shifting rock as it was possible to get, and Deke followed, still remembering to keep his gun in sight.

Slowly, the huge rocks above the escape tunnel slid into one another, toppling in a chain like a row of dominoes. With a loud crash, they fell upon the recent opening that Deke had made with his explosives and closed it solidly. The limestone dust filtered through the air and settled.

Deke's eyes widened almost comically with shock. Avidly, they searched the wall for the missing square of light that had marked the opening. An animal sound came from Deke's throat.

"Andrew!" shouted Chris. "Andrew must have sealed the hole!" His face was a mixture of jubilance and fear as he realized both the justice of it and the fact that the closing of the hole blocked their only means of escape.

With a sudden chill, Tom knew that the old miner had somehow gotten free and set another charge. Believing that his nephew had been responsible for the O'Reillys' deaths, he had sought the only justice available to him. Without realizing it, he had made things much more difficult. Tom turned and looked into the dangerously violent, fear-maddened eyes of Deke Mahler.

Deke roughly grabbed Tom by the shoulders in a sudden outburst of uncontrollable fear.

"You've been here hours before us! You've got to know another way out!"

Tom was not as heavy as Deke Mahler, but he was as tall. Their eyes met. "There's only one way left to go." He watched Deke's quick, hopeful expression. "The river."

Deke looked at the roaring, foaming river and paled. "What do you mean? I don't see a boat!"

Tom continued as if Deke hadn't spoken. "It meets the Pecos on the other side of that wall. That's the only escape route. There's an underwater tunnel we'll all have to swim through to make it out of here."

Deke looked as if he wanted to scream. "You're lying!" he whispered. "You're just saying that because you know . . . ." He looked wildly about and met the calm eyes of Chris O'Reilly.

Tom took Deke's wrists and tore them off his shoulders where the big man had been hanging on for dear life. He flung them aside with contempt and smiled grimly.

"Full circle, eh Deke? It took twenty-five years, but you're finally going to get those big feet wet. It will be interesting to see you swim that underwater channel weighted down with the treasure."

An image of the soldiers of the Spaniard, Cortez, trapped on a bridge to the Aztec city 450 years before and hindered in a losing battle by the uncomfortable weight of the gold, came to Chris's mind with the same sense of historical justice that drove his father's words.

"I can't swim!" Deke bellowed, his eyes wide with the imagined terror of finding himself underwater beneath crushing tons of rock.

"I know it." Tom's voice held his contempt.

Chris prepared himself for the outburst of violence he was sure would follow. Deke's eyes were wide and staring, and his movements became jerky. The mind which had controlled the body was yielding to a bottomless fear. At any moment, Chris knew, Deke would attack his father.

Still submerged in the nightmare of imagining himself underwater, Mahler raised his gun and waved it wildly. "I'll shoot if you don't get me out of here!" he threatened in a thick, clumsy voice. His breath came in quick gasps.

Suddenly, he stopped, a mad and crafty smile lighting his face. "No," he said thickly. "I don't have to die. One of you will swim out of here. You'll get my uncle to set another fuse! That's it," he said reassuringly to himself. "I'll give him twenty minutes." His voice rose into hysteria. "If there's not a hole in that wall in twenty minutes, I'll use this gun on the one who stays behind!"

Chris wondered if Deke's mind could weather the strain of being trapped for even twenty minutes. His rapidly progressing hysteria made it doubtful. But it didn't really matter. What he was demanding wasn't possible. It had taken Deke himself with Andrew's maps hours at least to blast that opening. It would take at least another hour to set and blast a new hole. Looking into Deke's bloodshot eyes, he knew he'd never get the man to listen to reason now. He looked down at the black, swirling river. A plan was forming in his mind, an idea born from desperation.

The voice of Andrew Mahler flashed through his mind telling him that he had sent two logs underwater through the channel and had recovered only one. He saw an image of a labyrinth of underwater dead ends hollowed out by the same force that had created the caves above. He shuddered with the feeling of walls close about his body like the inflexible hospitality of a grave.

He drew a deep breath. He knew he was infinitely more capable of swimming that channel than his father. He also knew that if he asked permission, he would never get it. There was no other way. With a quick shrug, he dropped the knapsack heavily behind him.

Just before the water closed over his head, he heard his father's anguished cry and Deke Mahler's brutal laugh.

It was dark, darker than anywhere Chris had ever been before. He felt his body caught and twisted against his will into strange, contorted shapes as the current gripped him. Occasionally, he hit against the top and sides of the channel, unable to control the force that sent him whirling out of control.

Shivers of pain flashed through his body as he slammed into a rock. He felt his courage all but disappear as terrible doubts filled his thoughts in the nightmare of the underwater channel. Had his decision to dive in been too quick? Would they have had a better chance if they had both jumped Deke and tried to take his gun away? Why had he acted so quickly? The horrible closeness of the rocky tunnel made him feel alone and helpless and afraid.

How far was it to freedom—fifty yards, five hundred? He felt his lungs bursting and remembered to release a tiny bit of air, lowering the pressure inside his chest. Would this tunnel never end? He couldn't stand much more. And then, just when he thought he had to take a breath or die, he was aware of a pale, gray light above him in the water and kicked fiercely up to break the surface and gasp his starved lungs full of air.

Outside, in the canyon, dawn had come. The calm and peaceful flowing of the Pecos River gave no evidence of the roaring turbulence inside the walls. Thirty feet away, slumped over the bank of the river, sat a dejected figure. Andrew. His white head was cradled in his arms in an attitude of utter hopelessness.

Chris swam over to the bank where Andrew sat unmoving. As he reached up for a hold on the rock, he saw a shudder run through the old man's body as he hesitantly raised his head, unable to believe that he had really seen one of the faces he most wanted to see in the world. His wrinkled old face, ravaged with grief, showed utter shock, the lack of expression that precedes a strong emotion. As he realized that what he saw was real, his face grew twenty years younger, serene and untroubled. His gnarled old hand reached strongly down and grasped Chris firmly as he clambered out of the river.

"Andrew!" gasped Chris. "We need your help." Quickly, he explained the situation.

The old miner nodded. "There's enough explosive left over to open ten walls, but it'll take more time than we have left even to figure out where to set the charge."

Chris looked at his watch. Miraculously, only five minutes had passed since he had dived into the river. He looked at Andrew. "Go ahead," he said. "Deke won't wait for you. He's crazy with fear. If nothing happens in the next fifteen minutes to change his mind, he'll shoot my father."

Andrew paled. "What are you going to do?"

Chris drew a deep breath. "I'm going to change his mind. There's only one way now." Briefly, he outlined his plan. It was dangerous and daring, and he saw a hundred objections in the old man's fearful eyes. His own mind whirled with reasons why he shouldn't do it, but he pushed them firmly aside.

It took Chris almost four minutes to run the boulder-strewn half mile to the cove where the Pecos threaded its violent way beneath the cliffs. He looked down at the darkest part of the river. Gently, the water swirled around, a vortex giving promise of a hidden turbulence below. He pulled off his shoes and sodden outer clothing, which he'd had no time to take off before. He felt lighter, less hampered now.

He put aside the thought that if he drowned, his father's life would be at the mercy of a madman. His breath grew quick as he remembered the inflexible closeness of the walls of rock. He shut his eyes and dived into the icy water.

Ten feet beneath the surface of the river, he felt himself being pulled inside as helpless as he had been before. He tried to shape his body like an arrow, hands joining before his head, streamlining his body. An arrow had a better chance than a bulky, flailing object to thread its way through the narrow channel ahead.

A sharp rock slashed his stomach, and involuntarily he jackknifed, bracing against the pain. Jerked off balance, he felt himself thrust whirling, head over heels, against a solid wall of rock. The current held him helpless there.

A solid wall of rock! He felt himself trapped in a blind alley of solid rock with little air left in his bursting lungs and a head that ached fiercely from a multitude of unseen blows.

He forced his panic-stricken mind to think. Strong currents of water swirled in powerful circles against his body. If this were a dead end and he were to be drowned, then he wouldn't feel the tug of the river at all. If it were a place of no return, then it would be a peaceful little cove, as quiet as a tomb. With sudden hope, he realized that this water was as furious as ever, still finding an outlet to the main channel somewhere nearby.

Straining his arms against the weight of rushing water, he reached out to both sides and touched two solid walls. He raised his head and bumped it against a low ceiling.

He gathered his oxygen-starved and weakening body for one last effort and thrust himself downward in a semi-somersault. He felt his body pass through into another channel and shoot forward, unobstructed. With the last vestiges of his conscious mind, he felt his head break the water. The stale air in his lungs exploded in a burst of sound, and a long, welcome breath of air filled them in a great gasp. Once again, he heard the echoing roar of the river, and he knew he was back in the cavern.

He was very tired. Treading water in a current as strong as this one was a near impossibility, so he allowed it to carry him along. If only Deke weren't facing toward the river! In his mind, he felt the angry sting of bullets.

The current pushed him around the high bank, and there they were, his father and Deke Mahler. Deke's back was to him as he impatiently faced the wall where Andrew was to set the charge.

With the remnants of his failing strength, Chris fought the current which drove him toward the far wall and swam diagonally toward the riverbank ten feet behind Deke Mahler.

The river ran two feet below the bank, and cautiously Chris raised his head above it. He saw Deke's right hand twitch nervously. The big man looked impatiently at his watch, and Chris took a deep breath. It must be almost time. A normal man would wait an hour longer if he believed there was a chance to escape, but Deke's mind was no longer sane. The macabre disappearance of his friends and his fear of water had driven him mad. He raised his gun toward Tom, and Chris hesitated no longer.

Unconcerned about being seen, he clawed his way out of the water. His yell of distraction was barely audible over the roar of the river. But catching the movement out of the corner of his eye, Deke whirled around. For one eternal moment, Chris had the chilling sensation that comes from looking down the cold, dark barrel of a gun, and then he became aware that the big man was falling toward him, the gun dropping from his hand.

Deke's mouth opened soundlessly with terror as he saw the course of his descent. Way off balance now, he fell blindly toward the river, Tom O'Reilly's shoving hands leaving his body as the weight of the stolen gold took over. With the muffled cry of a nightmare come to pass, Deke fell into the black, shining current and disappeared from sight.

Chris felt his father's hands pulling him to safety. The tension of knowing that he must succeed dropped away so quickly that sudden blackness clouded his vision, and he fell limply to his knees, unaware of the deep pride in his father's tender glance.

Soon, they heard the first of Andrew's attempts to blast into the cavern. They hurried over to the shelter of the tunnel and waited.

In half an hour, they heard Andrew's voice as he stuck his head through a small hole at the top of a fresh pile of rubble.

"Hey! You two loafers! Come and help me push away these rocks! Do you expect me to do all the work?"

Tom laughed and ran over to the opening. He pretended not to notice the tears of joy that ran down the old miner's face as he clasped his old friend's hand in greeting.

An hour later, accompanied by Andrew and his father, Chris looked back at the limestone cliffs above the Aztec caverns. Against the blue horizon of a new day, he saw the cougar's dark-gold silhouette. It would be only a matter of time before the Survivor came to meet the man who had been searching for him all his life. Chris had seen it in the Aztec's eyes that night. The Indian had at last snapped the spell of tradition and joined forces with them in the fight against Deke Mahler. This time, he wouldn't disappear. This time, Andrew and his father would meet him halfway, as they had failed to do so many times before. And if he failed to come, this time they would seek him out. Andrew's dream of a lifetime would soon come true.

He thought of Deke Mahler and his gang, whose greedy dreams had been thwarted by the actions of determined, honest men. He felt a sense of awe that the same kind of evil that had driven a tribe of hunted people to hide 450 years before had now provided the catalyst for the sole survivor of a long-lost tribe to emerge into the sunlight after centuries of darkness, to live as a human being.